A PURPOSE TO OUR SAVAGERY

FOURTEEN STORIES

TOMAS BAIZA

RIZE

CONTENTS

Paperback 978-1-955062-41-1
Ebook 978-1-955062-42-8

1
NEZAHUALCÓYOTL

"Dani. Dani?"

    Several people turn to stare. Alma curses under her breath, certain that they can hear the fear in her voice.

"Dani!" It's there now, she knows, in full display. Weakness masquerading as anger. She listens for the bells. It's not that she doesn't hear any. Just the opposite. There are hundreds—thousands—of them, ringing out from every direction.

"No, no, no," Alma says under her breath. "How could I have been so stupid"

A squadron of Tiny Tot dancers bounces past, their animated voices spiraling with the jangle of their regalia. On the far side of the concessions area, the loudest drum circle thus far announces itself with a new round of thunder. High falsettos ride a pentatonic melody. Now Alma can barely make out the bells she didn't want to hear, let alone the four she does.

Shaking hands climb her scalp to the top of her head. Thick hair spears outward through her fingers like ebony lightning strikes. "Jesus, Dani. Where are you?"

She had only looked away for a second.

* * *

"¡Dani, vente p'acá! C'mon little man, show your tías my invention."

The boy burst from his bedroom and galloped down the hallway into the kitchen, an ear-to-ear grin lighting up his freckled face. Tied to the laces of his black Chuck Taylors were four bells that sounded like miniature Christmases on fast-forward. He leaped through the air and crashed into Raquel's lap. Alma's sisters roared with laughter.

"¡Ay!" Raquel grunted as she hefted Dani. "You're getting big! How old are you, twenty?"

"I'm this many!" Dani shouted, holding up four fingers.

Alma's breath caught at the contrast between Dani's and Raquel's hair. Loose blonde curls smothered in her sister's blue-black mane.

"Sis, bells are for baby shoes! He's too old for those," Raquel laughed. She let her nephew squirm to the floor. Dani sped from the kitchen, bells ringing down the hallway and back into his bedroom.

"No he's not," said Alma. "Besides, you been shopping with him lately? He booked on me at K-Mart last Saturday and then later on at the Flea Market. He's like The Flash. The only way I found him was because of the bells." Alma pulled three beers out of the refrigerator and set them down on the small kitchen table "God," she whispered, "what if I had lost him?"

Raquel took two beers from Alma. "You should get one of those things we saw at the mall. What are those chingaderas called? Un lazo, a leash."

"¡Una correa! Gah! Your Spanish is worse than your English." Maribel accepted a bottle from Raquel.

"Shut up," said Raquel, the hint of a smile betraying her frown.

"No way I'm putting one of those child-leashes on my son," Alma said. "Let the gabacha soccer moms walk their kids like dogs."

* * *

Alma scans the crowd, inner panic clawing at the calm facade. Keep it together, girl, she warns herself. You don't want to be remembered as Chicana-Who-Lost-Her-Shit at the Stanford Powwow. Alma could feel her face hardening, clamping down.

Her Mexican Face, Bill used to call it.

"Women's Traditional dancers to the arena please. Women's Traditional to the arena. Ten minutes, ladies," a male voice announces over the PA speakers.

The fail-safe to Dani's bells were his red and white flare pants, the idea being that the kid was always moving and the hideous stripes would be as noticeable as the bells. But everywhere Alma looks she sees color. Flags and banners and blankets and regalia. Dani's pants could be right in front of her and she'd miss them in the chromatic tsunami.

Alma takes several quick steps then stops short to keep from being trampled. Women's Traditional dancers file past on their way to the arena. Shawls, tassels, feather fans, bead and silver work. A tightness creeps into Alma's throat. Young, old, skinny, fat, lithe, lumbering—the women file by as a group. Some laugh and chatter excitedly with fellow competitors, others are solemn, as if in meditation. Some, mostly younger, look like they want to puke.

Alma pulls at her hair waiting for the dancers to pass. Her mother had always complained about her hair. "Diós, m'ija, I can't do anything with this," she'd moan in Spanish, trying without success to wrestle Alma's cable-like strands into curlers. "I should leave you at the fairgrounds the next time those damn savages come. They'd know what to do with this mess!" Alma couldn't count the times her mother threatened to abandon her to aquellos malditos salvajes when they came to Flagstaff for the annual summer gathering, before Raquel and Maribel were born and the family had moved to California.

She remembers when she was old enough to understand that her mother's threats were really fear cowering behind hatred. Indians as boogeymen. Everyone needs someone to shit on, Alma thinks. Even us.

"Beautiful, aren't they."

Alma flinches. Two tall women stand next to her, admiring the dancers.

"Yeah, they are," Alma says, distracted. Her dark eyes scan the crowd for Dani. Still nothing. I need to move, she scolds herself. Scenarios—the things you read about in newspapers— begin to sprout like weeds in her mind. She turns to the women. "Excuse me, but—"

"How come you're not out there? You look like you could kick up some dust, girl," the first woman asks.

"Wh?—I—I don't dance."

"Well, you should," the second says. "You'd look good! What tribe are you anyways?"

"Tribe?" Alma mutters. "I'm not—"

Wait, aren't I? Sort of? What am I here?

"I'm Mexican. Chicana," Alma says.

The first woman's eyes narrow into slits as she stares at the passing dancers. A barely audible hiss slides through her teeth before she walks away.

Alma watches the woman disappear into the crowd, her face burning with anger.

"Excuse my sister," the second woman says. "She can be like that. Kinda mean."

Shame spreads through Alma's chest. She cringes at the

4

memory of her own sisters' faces when she lost her composure last night. My God, the things I said in front of them, she thinks. How could they not think I'm totally crazy now?

"Thank you," Alma says. "I have sisters, too. They can be hard." Alma's anguish vibrates inside her, swelling in intensity until it starts to shake itself apart. Oh fuck, don't cry in front of this woman, she commands herself.

The woman nods and leans forward to stare into Alma's eyes. "Hey, we don't know each other, but you look worried. Are you okay?"

"I'm looking for my son," Alma says haltingly. "He was just with me and now he's gone." She describes Dani down to his freckles.

"Bells on his shoes and striped hippy pants?" the woman says. "You sure you're not Indian?"

Alma curses herself as a single tear jumps down her round cheek. "Please, have you seen him?"

"No, but hey, kids go missing at these all the time. Been there, done that. They'll be gone for hours and turn up smelling like fry bread and piss. Prolly the worst part isn't that they were lost, but realizing they didn't miss you the whole time they were gone." She continues when Alma doesn't laugh. "Hey, look, I don't normally tell other women to actually go to the police, but there's a couple of Stanford cops at that tent over there, under those trees. They might be able to help. One of 'em's even sorta cute," the woman adds with a wink.

"Okay. Thanks. Good idea." Alma wipes her cheek and turns to leave.

"Hey," the woman says quickly. "The next time one of us asks which tribe you are, just lie. How the hell would we know?"

* * *

"Mami, will there be drums tomorrow?"

The semi-dark made Dani's whispers more intimate. Alma wanted nothing more than to crawl into bed with him and whisper back and forth until he fell asleep. A warm, dark, easy world just for the two of them. She pulled the covers up to his chin and mussed his hair. "How did you know there would be drums?" Dani had never been to a powwow.

"I saw it on TV last night. The Indians were drumming. They danced in a circle and there were feathers."

Alma shook her head in the dark. I can't believe I let him watch that John Wayne shit, she thought. Bill loved Westerns.

"Yeah, there will be drums," she whispered, stroking his cheek. "They're awesome. It won't be like on TV, though. The drums fill the air, m'ijo." She reached beneath the covers and placed a hand on his chest. "It's like the pounding comes from inside you."

Dani's eyes went wide in the dark. "Like your heart?"

"Bigger," Alma whispered. She kissed Dani on the forehead. "Duérmete, 'kay?" Halfway to the door she stumbled on his little shoes making the bells ring out.

"Mami."

"¿Qué, m'ijo?"

"Will I be big?"

"¿Cómo qué 'big'?"

"Will I be big, like Daddy?"

Alma pushed Dani's shoes aside with her foot. The bells tinkled in the dark. "Probably, m'ijo. Your abuelo was a big man."

"No, like Daddy?"

"God dammit, Dani, you'll be big, alright?" Alma snapped, her sudden anger filling the room like smoke. She stood near the door until the boy's sniffles reached her in the dark. Alma closed her eyes and sighed. She went to the bed and pulled him

6

to her. The boy's head shook against her chest. "You'll be what you need to be, m'ijo. I promise. Let's just think about the drums tomorrow, 'kay?"

"Ring my bells again when you go, Mami," Dani said and rolled away from her.

* * *

In the kitchen, Raquel and Maribel had gotten into the Lancers.

"Hey! That was for decoration," Alma scolded.

"Since when did you get so fancy that you use wine bottles for decoration?" Raquel said. "You pick that up in college?"

"I know, how bougie, right?" Maribel poured some wine in a coffee mug and passed it to Alma. "Everything okay in there?" she asked, glancing at Raquel. "We heard you and Dani just now."

Alma spun her mug slowly on the table. "Oh, it's fine. Dani misses Bill."

Raquel and Maribel nodded and sipped their wine.

"Soooo," Raquel cooed. She raised her mug to her lips and looked over the brim at Maribel.

Alma knew her younger sisters' tones, expressions, and body language better than they did themselves. "What."

"How come you been so weird lately?" Raquel asked.

Maribel smacked her lips on the wine. "You haven't been coming over to Mom's on Sundays."

"Or to church, or my birthday party, or cousin Monica's quinceañera," Raquel added.

"I've been busy," Alma said, cradling her mug.

"Yeah, busy being all reclusive and mysterious," said Maribel.

7

"You hiding a man from us or something?" Raquel asked, half-serious.

"Since when did you two get so metiche?" Alma raised her mug and drained it. "I've just been wanting time to myself."

Raquel rolled her eyes. "So you'll go to a powwow tomorrow instead of hanging out with family?"

"What will you do there?" Maribel asked. "Eat weird shit like bison tacos?"

"I think she's going to meet someone," Raquel cut in. "That's it, huh, Sis. You don't want to risk a Mexican so you're looking for some Sioux warrior to ride up and sweep you off your feet."

"Yeah," Maribel said. "White guy didn't pan out, so you're swinging hard the other way, right past Mexican to Indian."

"¡Cállate el hocico ya, pendeja!" Alma summoned the voice she had perfected tongue-lashing her sisters when they were younger, the same one she used on Bill to spook him. Maribel's eyes welled up and Raquel aimed an imploring look at her older sister. Alma lowered her head in a silent apology. "Jesus, you two," she said through clenched teeth. "I shoulda drowned you in the tub when I had the chance."

Raquel threw her head back and laughed. Alma reached out to wipe a tear from Maribel's cheek and cupped her chin. "That mouth of yours, Mari," she said.

The sisters sipped port from their coffee mugs in silence. After a few minutes, Raquel drew a breath of courage and dared to look Alma in the eye. "¿Entonces...qué buscas?"

"Yeah, Sis," Maribel added. "What are you looking for?"

* * *

Alma hesitates, steels herself, and approaches the police tent. Under the shelter two uniformed officers sit heavily on crooked folding chairs. Two walkie-talkies sit on the picnic table in front of them.

Alma's hopes swell when she sees that one of them has dark skin and thick black hair. The maybe-Latino nods vaguely at Alma as she approaches. She takes note of his name tag. ORTIZ.

Tranquílate, Alma tells herself. Stay calm. Don't let these payasos think you're hysterical.

"Excuse me. I'm looking for my son. His name is Dani. Daniel," she says, making sure to accent his name. "He was just with me and now he's gone. Curly, light hair. Blue eyes. Red and white pants and bells on his shoes. Can you help me find him?"

Ortíz glances at his companion, a Ken-doll look-alike who seems more interested in the passing female dancers than missing children. Ortíz turns back to Alma. "Have you looked for him?"

Alma blinks. "Explain to me, please, how I could possibly know that my son was missing if I hadn't already looked for him."

"Ha! Got you there, Art!" says Ken-doll.

Ortíz frowns at his partner and then returns his glare to Alma. "Have you spoken with the Powwow Director? Just tell him your tribe and he'll take care of you. What tribe are you anyways?" he asks, gesturing at Alma's turquoise bracelets.

Alma sets her hands on the picnic table and leans towards Ortíz. "Tú y yo somos de la misma tribu, carnal," says Alma. You and I are from the same tribe, dude.

"Joke's on you, Miss," Ken-doll chuckles. "Officer Ortíz here doesn't speak a lick of es-pan-yol, do you, Art?" Ken-doll elbows Ortíz from his folding chair. "What would you call that? Not an 'apple.' That's Indian. Or an 'Oreo.' That's a n—." He snaps his mouth shut and fiddles with one of the walkie-talkies.

Alma stares at Ken-doll impassively, the word pocho settling into a corner of her brain. Not quite the same type of food-based slur as 'apple' or 'Oreo,' but close enough. Pocho: faded, rotten, spoiled. A Mexican who'd lost their language or culture.

Ortíz sits, sour-faced and unable to look at either Alma or his partner.

Alma places two hands flat on the picnic table. "Hey, are either of you going to help me find my son or what?"

Ken-doll stands up and shoves a hand into his cop belt. "Don't worry, Miss. We must get a dozen lost kids a day at things like this," he says, waiving his walkie-talkie around his head. "I'll radio our guys to keep an eye out. Can you describe him again?"

Alma hurriedly describes Dani to Officer Ken-doll while watching Ortíz. For all of her fear, she feels an urge to tell Ortíz that it's okay, to remind him that there are no litmus tests for Chicanos. No blood quantum requirements or reservations. She wants to tell him that Dani himself is half-white. That he would always be made to feel incomplete. She's tempted to tell Ortíz that Dani is a whole person. As is she. Even dickhead Ortíz.

"Miss? Miss?"

Ken-doll's face hovers in front of her. "Whoa, lost you there, cutie. So, I'll radio our guys and we'll keep an eye out. Meantime, I'd recommend you go to that big tent way the hell over there, by the dancing arena. Talk to Leonard. Leonard..." Ken-doll snaps his fingers. "The hell is Leonard's last name, Art?"

"Three Bears," Ortíz mumbles.

"Seriously? The Powwow Director's last name is Three Bears? You couldn't make that stuff up," Ken-doll says, shaking his head. He inspects Alma with sudden interest and digs into his chest pocket, just next to his badge. "Leonard Three Bears is running this circus. He's the man with the mic and can make an announcement." From his pocket, Ken-doll produces a business card. "Here you go, Miss. You make sure to give me a call if you need anything. Anything at all."

Alma takes the card between two fingers, as one might hold a dried dog turd. "Very kind of you, officer," she says, lips curled. She leans around Ken-doll. "Oye, Arturo," she says to Ortíz. "No te rajes, güey. It's not too late for you."

* * *

The apartment balcony faced eastward across 680. A mile beyond the freeway, the Diablo Foothills rose golden and velvety in the early summer evening, their creases filled with dark lines of black oaks and eucalyptus.

Maribel snored softly on the wicker couch, her head resting on Raquel's lap. Raquel stroked her sister's hair absentmindedly. She took another sip of Lancers and watched Alma gaze at the foothills. Alma's handsome face held an inscrutable restlessness that could make others uneasy. More striking than beautiful, she wielded a heavy presence that had always made her sisters fall in line. Alma had essentially raised her and Maribel. Guided, pulled, and hammered them through the rough spots. Rivals, boys, men, pregnancy scares—and not-scares—their parents, money. Sometimes Raquel wondered which was worse—the fuck ups or suffering Alma's wrath for screwing up in the first place. Still, their big sister had gotten them through it all. Raquel knew that if the world went up in flames, Alma would be the last one standing, stone-faced with a garden hose in her hand.

Now it was their big sister's turn to need fixing and neither she nor Maribel had the first clue what to do.

"¿De qué 'stás pensando?" Raquel asked, brushing Maribel's thick hair with her fingers. She hoped that asking in Spanish might disarm her sister.

Alma smiled wistfully. "I'm thinking about how if you concentrate hard enough, you can almost convince yourself that the highway sounds like the ocean and the foothills are huge waves."

"Is that why you been so moody? You want to move to Santa Cruz? Let your legs go all Sasquatch and become a granola girl?"

Alma smirked at her sister and looked again to the foothills. She marveled at how they somehow held onto the daytime, as though the golden grasses absorbed sunlight and gave it back long after night had fallen. "Jíjole, could you imagine me in Birkenstocks?"

"Nope, and if you stop shaving your sobacos I'm telling Mom. So, what then? Ever since you kicked Bill out, it's like you've been only half here, like a ghost. I know it's not because you miss him, right?"

"My God, Raquel. No! Getting rid of Bill was the best thing I ever did for myself—and for Dani, even if he doesn't know it yet. And don't ask me again if I'm trying to find a man. I'm not."

"Okay," said Raquel, frustrated. "¿Entonces qué?"

Alma looked to the hills again. "I didn't think it would be a big deal marrying a white guy," she said. "I thought we'd have kids. They'd look like both of us. Pretty stupid, huh?"

"Look on the bright side," Maribel groaned, sitting up and rubbing her temples with her palms. "Dani could do a lot worse than look like Bill. That whiteboy may have been an asshole, but he was fine, Sis. Dani's light hair and blue eyes... ¡wáchale!"

Raquel nodded in agreement. "Seriously, you're gonna

need to lock that boy up when he gets older. Last thing you want is some chonga girl deciding he's her future."

Maribel squinted. "Ay, your prissy dessert wine snuck up on me."

The glow of the foothills had begun to fade. Alma watched as the last of the gold in the grasses turned a deep red and then a bruised purple. She closed her eyes and, for just a moment, wished she could rise from her chair, float out over the highway, and fly past those hills to some place where who you were was clear, nothing to negotiate or bargain for, to promote or defend.

Alma forced herself back to earth, there on the patio with her sisters. "Have either of you ever thought about who we are? About where we come from?"

* * *

"Fancy Shawl dancers to the arena please. Fancy Shawl dancers, ten minutes to start. Thank you!"

The Powwow Director is a tall older man. His striped Western shirt fits snugly over his barrel chest and Alma wonders whether he had to have jeans custom made to bend around his bowed legs. He sets the microphone down on the picnic table serving as his desk and tucks his clipboard under his arm. "How can I help you, Miss?"

"Leonard Three Bears?"

"The one and only," Leonard grins.

"Good." Alma slaps Ken-doll's card on the table. "My son's lost and they told me that you could help me find him."

Leonard lifts the card to just beneath his nose and inspects it under his glasses. "Ah, the Great White Hope actually gave you this? That guy..." he says, shaking his head.

"Can you make an announcement?" Alma asks, hating the fear in her voice.

Leonard pulls a pencil from behind his ear. "Of course. What's your boy's name?"

"Daniel," says Alma.

Leonard looks up, confused. "Danielle?"

"Dan-iel," Alma repeats slowly, in her clearest Spanish accent. "He also goes by Dani."

"Donny?"

"Dah-ni."

"Thonny?" Leonard scratches his head.

"Daniel!" Alma throws her hands up in frustration. "He—just...Daniel. He'd recognize Daniel. People call him that all the time."

"Okay," says Leonard, relieved. "How old is he?"

"Four."

"Ah, that's gonna be a problem," Leonard says, running his hand over his face. "I've found that the younger kids don't tend to listen to the announcements. And even if they did, they'd have trouble finding their way to our tent. That's why they're lost in the first place, right?" He holds up his hands at Alma's panicked expression. "Now, it's alright. Just tell me what he's wearing and his name and I can make the announcement that he's lost and whoever finds him can bring him here."

"Wait, I—" Alma jams the heels of her palms into her temples. "I hadn't thought this through. Are you telling me you're going to announce to thousands of people that my son is lost and tell them all his name and exactly what he looks like? Anyone could run off with him."

"Miss, there's no way that would happen. This is...there are good people here."

"I didn't mean anything by that. I've seen a lot of really bad stuff. I just want—." Alma falls silent, her reserves all but spent.

"Miss, I—" Leonards starts to say, but is silenced by an eruption of drums from across the dance arena. "Ah, shit

14

on a stick!" he yells, looking at his watch. "Those Owl Rib guys weren't supposed to start for another five minutes."

Alma leans on the folding table, her almond eyes wide and unseeing. "The drums," she whispers.

"Beg pardon, Miss?" says Leonard, his voice raised.

"The drums!" Alma shouts, a smile spreading across her face.

"Yeah, I know!" Leonard yells and looks over his shoulder, "Somebody go tell those guys to knock it off until their scheduled start or I'm 'bout to pull their complementary meal tickets real quick."

"No, don't! Thank you, Mr. Three Bears. Thank you!"

"You're welcome, but I din't—" is all Alma hears when she rushes from the tent.

Her path takes her straight across the ground where the Fancy Shawl dancers are hurriedly gathering, surprised by the sudden start of the drums. The women who see Alma coming manage to step aside in swirls of satin tassels. Some shoot her annoyed looks, others smile or laugh at her headlong sprint across the dance arena.

* * *

Raquel squinted at Alma. "Huh? What do you mean?"

"You heard me. Who we are. Where we come from." said Alma, exasperated.

"Um, yeah," Raquel mocked. "We're from The Saddle— you know, the barrio just south of downtown? Where all of us grew up?"

Maribel pointed at Alma. "And where the Ramírezes' chicken coop caught fire and me and Raquel couldn't go out into the alley to watch because you had cut our hair with pinking shears to get back at us for snitching on you for sneaking out at night."

"I know where we grew up, Raquel. And you both deserved it for ratting me out. No," Alma shifted in her chair, gazing out at the dark foothills. "I mean our place in all of this. Mexican, white, Chicana, mestiza, pocha, coconut—whatthe-fuckever. Don't you ever think about those things?"

"Not like you," her sisters said in unison.

Maribel shook the empty Lancer's bottle and set it down again. "C'mon, Sis. ¿De nuevo con ésto? You think about this shit too much."

"We're definitely not white," said Alma, ignoring Maribel.

"No, we're not," Raquel said, annoyed. "We're Mexican."

"Are we, though? Really?" Alma said, turning to her sisters. "Since when has Mom ever called us that? She doesn't think we are. All of us were born on this side. How many of the people we actually know and socialize with are from Mexico?"

"Nobody," Maribel said. "Mexicans are the ones who love to remind us we're not Mexican. They're always correcting our Spanish. They say weird shit like '¡Qué chafa!' and 'la neta' They call us 'pochas' or 'vendidas' and we call them 'mojados.'"

Raquel frowned. "Wait a minute, I say 'la neta.'"

"I know, pero we love you anyways," said Maribel.

Maribel eyed Alma. "Well, you went to college, so that officially makes you the whitest of all of us."

"And what did she major in?" Raquel chimed in. "Latino Studies! Mami still goes on about that. What did that get you, Sis?"

"It got my ass graduated," Alma said, her voice dangerously low.

"Yeah, and you dated all those weird activist man-boys with those dumbass Aztec nicknames," Maribel said, undaunted. "Moctezuma and Cuauhtémoc and that kind of shit."

"Those are real Mexican names," Alma said, staring out at the foothills again, "from before the Spaniards came and called us things like 'Alma,' 'Raquel,' and 'Maribel.' From when we used to pray to different gods."

"And eat children's hearts! Na-ah, Sis. Count me out," Maribel laughed.

Alma closed her eyes and breathed deeply. "When I first knew I'd have a boy, I wanted to name him Nezahualcóyotl."

Raquel rolled her eyes. "Oh, Bill would have loved that!"

"Nezawhatl? The hell does that even mean?" asked Maribel.

Alma turned toward her sisters and held them with her eyes, dark and heavy. "Last week, just before I lost Dani at K-Mart, some woman—a white woman—asked me if I was looking for any more children to take care of. I was confused and asked her what she was talking about. She pointed at Dani and said 'For babysitting. Are you taking any more children on?'" Alma dragged a hand across her wet cheek. "Dani and I look so different, she thought I was his babysitter or nanny or something. I looked at him and saw this beautiful blonde-haired, blue-eyed boy and asked myself how the hell he could be mine. I went kind of crazy for a second and wondered whether he actually was mine. Right then, it was like I'd lost my son and had no idea how I'd find him again, how I'd get him back."

Alma buried her face in her hands. "I can't do this," she said between sobs. "I don't know how I'm going to raise a white boy. A white man. I'm afraid I'm going to screw him up so bad."

Raquel and Maribel looked at one another and cautiously moved to either side of Alma. Raquel dared to take her older sister's hand while Maribel ran her fingers through Alma's hair. Neither spoke.

Alma sat limp between her sisters. "Hungry Coyote," she said, gulping air.

Raquel leaned in close. "What, Sis?"

"Nezahualcóyotl," Alma said, her voice hollow. "It means Hungry Coyote."

Alma emerges from the tangle of dancers and almost crashes into several men seated in a circle. They lean over a massive drum and their long sticks rise and fall in unison. One man's clear voice rings out first and is followed by the rest.

Past the drum circle, something catches Alma's eye. Red and white stripes. A bouncing mop of blonde hair. Every glimpse of Dani between passersby is like the fall of a drumstick, the fragile shell of calm she'd managed to maintain cracking beneath the blows. Walking slowly around the drum circle, relief floods Alma's body and her eyes spill over. With the tears comes the guilt—for having let him out of her sight, for not keeping him close.

Alma walks into the open and her breath catches at the sight of her son. Immune to dizziness or distraction, Dani spins, arms outstretched and feet kicking up clouds of fine dust. As he turns, Alma could swear the tiny bells on his shoes become louder, competing with the thunderous BOOM-boom-boom-boom behind her. Her knees weaken and she falls onto her backside in the dirt while Dani turns and shakes. She can hear them clearly, the tinkling shoelace bells now ayoyote rattles on his ankles and wrists announcing every footfall, declaring to friend and foe the presence of someone to be reckoned with. With each rotation, his flint-bladed macuahuitl traces an arc through the air. Alma shouts in surprise when, in his next turn, Dani produces a deerskin shield emblazoned with the swirling ollin, its nexus symbolizing movement and transformation. Before her eyes, her son grows taller, more beautiful and imposing. Tiny arms swell into corded muscle as shield and flint-club meet enemies on all sides, every whoosh of the weapon a warning and promise. Across Dani's broad chest hangs a necklace of human hearts pumping gore down shining stomach and legs. Alma swoons and throws her hands out to keep from collapsing. A canine muzzle flashes before her, its upper teeth casting a jagged shadow across Dani's black-painted face. The coyote helmet's fur bristles in the hot, dry air.

Never, not in any fantasy or nightmare, has Alma ever seen such a perfect being, an entity so exquisitely equipped to fight, to be who he must.

"Now you're big, m'ijo," Alma gasps. "Big as you'll ever need to be."

Alma pushes herself to her feet. Dani, so close to her now, spins and sways and stamps the dirt, raises his shield to meet the arrows, rocks, and spears that will inevitably come.

Let him fight, Alma wills, hands balled into fists.

Let him never be what I would have made him.

2

HOLE

The hole in the sidewalk was not especially deep, perhaps only six or seven feet from street level to the bottom. Nevertheless, when one is falling at a forty-five degree angle, fingers and toes splayed and seeking contact with any hard surface, it might as well be bottomless for that half-second.

Claudia clutched her bag as sore feet slipped from her new sandals.

* * *

She'd bought the sandals that morning, still jet lagged from her red-eye to Mexico City. The shop was just a block from the apartment her dissertation advisor let her rent for the summer. The apartment had two bedrooms, her advisor had said. Maybe he'd come for a few days in August, he'd suggested, when her research was wrapping up and she had some time to spare. Claudia barely stifled the eyeroll. She couldn't risk losing the inexpensive apartment when her fellowship didn't pay a summer stipend. Best to worry about him later.

Colonia Parroquia was a safe neighborhood according to her advisor and all the travel guides. Claudia was relieved to find it quiet and even quaint, in that pragmatic Mexican way that made allowances for the occasional proletarian grumbling or dusting of volcanic ash from Popocatépetl. Safe enough for her to decide to take a long walk. It would be good, she reasoned, to get out and absorb the city before she spent the rest of the summer barricaded in archives and libraries.

Buying the sandals made no practical sense other than to instill a sense of purpose, something to distract her from the anxiety of dislocation and the occasional emptiness that seemed to crouch always on the periphery. That and she knew she had nice feet. Claudia felt a small thrill to think that Mexican men might notice those feet as she walked the city.

Not that she would talk to any of those men. It was one thing to be noticed, but another thing altogether to engage. No, she would make sure to stay unencumbered this trip.

It surprised Claudia as she fell, her body rotating to face-up and approaching perpendicular, how perfectly rectangular the hole was. The perimeter of its slick dirt walls exactly matched the missing slab of sidewalk above. She had just noticed that the scalloped texture of the cement ended when she heard the high voice behind her. An instant before she felt the shove, she looked over her shoulder into the face of the President of Mexico, Carlos Salinas de Gortari.

Claudia's handsome feet ached in her new sandals.

She had set her face to impassive, to mask the pain, and

made sure to stay on the larger streets. When a man smiled or commented, she would let her mouth curl slightly upward at the corners, her lips pressing into the ghost of a smile. Better a modest, non-committal acknowledgement than outright rejection. She didn't want any trouble.

To Claudia's delight, she found a bookstore on Fray Servando, a broad, busy street that would eventually give way to Avenida Chapultepec. It smelled like any other bookstore, though she was caught off guard by the sheer number of little books in such a cramped space. Browsing the stacks, Claudia realized it was because there were almost no hard-bound publications, but rather hundreds of delicate, poorly constructed paperbacks, their pages thin as rice paper. Her pulse quickened when she found *El Colegio Real de las Doncellas Ynditas* and *La Historia de la Educación de México Precolombiano*, both of which she'd seen cited but were not in her university's holdings.

The middle-aged clerk was so pleased that Claudia spoke Spanish, –¡y con muy poco acento inglés!– the woman gushed. Claudia thanked her, red-faced, and carefully placed her new books in her shoulder bag. The bookseller patted Claudia's arm, thanking her for her purchase, and added in her cultured Chilango accent, –Señorita, make sure to wrap those tightly. They're delicate and might not travel well.–

Claudia instinctively clamped down on her bag, the square corners of the books shoving into her bare underarm. In these busy milliseconds, her mind did not register the pain, but rather relief at their proximity. Body rotating in the air, Claudia's eyes caught the top of the president's bald head just cresting the edge of the pavement like a moonrise against storm clouds.

* * *

Avenida Chapultepec took her southwest towards Chapultepec Park.

Cha-pul-te-pec!

Claudia repeated those exquisite syllables again and again as she perused the storefronts.

Chapultepec. Grasshopper Hill.

What luminous, inspired soul first came upon that place and gave it that name? Was that person a poet, someone from whom such beauty was expected? Or was that understanding of a place's essential nature ubiquitous amongst a people who fought to survive every day and whose connection to this world was more practical, more sincere?

Distracted by such thoughts, Claudia found herself deep in the park, sharing its wide paths with couples and families. Casually, she watched them, hand-in-hand, gifting one another with affection. Some of the couples were women, their arms linked as they spoke and laughed, a signal to men that they intended to enjoy one another's company and need not be bothered. Claudia had forgotten about this tradition and felt a tug at her heart. She wished she had a girlfriend to spend the day with.

There it was again—that occasional weakening of resolve, a subtle tug at her chest she refused to acknowledge as longing.

* * *

Claudia worried about what the mud at the bottom of the hole would do to her books and sandals. The uneven dirt floor was pock marked with shallow puddles from the earlier rain, each pool reflecting the slate gray sky above like a dead eye. Hadn't she seen a *lavandería* near the apartment?

* * *

She had forgotten about the mid-afternoon monsoons.

Every summer afternoon, storm clouds climbed into the ring over the great basin of central Mexico and wrestled one another for dominance. Thunder would roll across the valley as twenty-one million people went about their daily business. When the skies finally opened up, like a god tripping over a brimming bucket, those twenty-one million people would act as though it was the first time it had ever rained in the history of Tenochtitlán and break into a wild sprint for the nearest Metro station.

Claudia had just given half her lunch—ten tacos for a peso! —to two children when the skies spilled over. She laughed and ran to cower behind a stone statue, and laughed even harder when she realized the statue was Tlaloc, the goggle-eyed god of rain. Sheltered by Tlaloc's hulking shoulders, she curved her lean body around her shoulder bag and stood on a raised curb to keep from soaking her new sandals.

When the rain ended fifteen minutes later, Claudia decided it was time to start back. She would take the Paseo de la Reforma.

* * *

A part of her brain—the untethered part that always ran and watched from a safe space when something bad happened— knew he wasn't really the president.

Probably because of the storm, Reforma was almost deserted, Claudia found herself all but alone on the normally bustling thoroughfare. The city smelled new, and birds that she hadn't noticed before now called out from palms and other trees she couldn't identify. She reminded herself to stop by a library and look up trees of the city, or maybe she would make a friend at the archives, a fellow researcher or local who would know which trees produced such deep red flowers.

The voice itself didn't frighten her, but she knew that it shouldn't have been there, not so unexpectedly. Without even time to freeze, she registered a change in the pattern of the sidewalk, the orange safety cones tossed aside, as she turned to look over her shoulder. President Salinas de Gortari was much shorter than she'd imagined. She'd seen him on television and knew he was Harvard educated, but surely a grown man was taller than that?

And his face was made of rubber.

It was the eyes that gave him away. Eyes within eyes, or rather, eyes within empty sockets. Through her brain flashed images of Xipe Totec, the hideous Flayed Lord, monster-god of renewal and rebirth whose priests would don the skin of their sacrifices, quivering, boneless hands and feet dangling from sycophants' limbs, gaping holes pulling at wide eyes and seeping lips. A sloughing off of the old and dripping arrival into a new, raw vulnerability.

Before Claudia could react, the masked boy placed his hands on the small of her back and shoved her into the gap in the sidewalk.

* * *

Claudia stood in the bottom of the hole, fists clenched, her bare feet set wide apart to keep from slipping in the mud. Above, a diminutive President Salinas de Xipe Totec peered over the edge. Against the churning gray clouds, Claudia saw the silhouette of a long knife. The president-monster-god pointed the blade at Claudia's bag which rested on its side, splattered in filth in a corner of her dirt cell.

His voice was high and clear as a castrato's.

–Qué hueco, Señorita. La bolsa, por favor.–

3
LOVE RITUAL

V elvety cheeks, silken eyebrows, two impossibly soft lips.
Everything your fingers explore is so achingly close to
perfection.

The room is silent, except for the officious beeping and
thrum of machines. Wispy shuffling in your peripheral. Words
are unthinkable, profane.

There are no windows or clocks. It is impossible to know
the time of day or to care. Time has no meaning here. Not
anymore.

Everyone wears masks, pulled high over mouths and noses,
only eyes exposed. One of the half-faces is crying, her throat
gurgling and blue paper mask soiled by tears and snot. Most of
the rest have turned away or try to act busy.

No one will look at you, and still everyone manages to
watch.

You shut your eyes against the odors—cold, biting, antiseptic—that are supposed to instill confidence that everything
will work out fine, that the experts had this covered, that this
could never go very, very wrong. So wrong that the sterile

promises claw past your clenched teeth and build a tangled, sour nest in your mouth.

Now you know that lies taste worse than white chocolate.

Yet the lies cannot ruin the most glorious smell of this world: newborn hair. Rich, human, and necessary. Hair so fine and light as atoms that it might as well be smoke easing past your lips.

Unencumbered by reason, you mumble a song your mother sang to you as a lullaby, a song from the Mexican Revolution about a woman too comfortable in the presence of men. You give it as an offering because it is the only piece of your heritage you can think of in your madness. The very idea of your voice not being the last thing he hears might send you through a window—if only there were any. You tell yourself it's okay because, no matter the lyrics, your mother gave you this song out of love. One of her rituals.

And so, you will choke down the salt of your rage and repeat that ritual, here, in this hateful place. You will do it because, more than anything else, you must leave love.

4
EXTRA-LARGE FOR THE LORD

We may ignore, but we can nowhere evade the presence of God. The world is crowded with Him. He walks everywhere incognito.

— *C.S. LEWIS*

J oey, tragically White and clueless. Joey who's in my English and P.E. classes, but thank God not Trigonometry or Health. Joey who yanks the half-burnt order ticket out from under the sizzling pizza. He squints at it and twists up his face, pale fingers wrapped round the intercom mic.

Beyond him, a packed dining room of Friday-night customers.

"Hurry up, dude," I say, super-heated pizzas rotating past my face, each time around smokier than the last.

Joey's frown sinks in deeper. "This name..." he says.

Crowding the hulking gas oven are fifteen pizzas on dual rotating decks. I have zero doubt that Dante Alighieri's editor made him remove the chapter where he declared the cramped kitchen of a strip mall pizza restaurant as one of the lowest levels of Hell. I sigh and slide the wood-handled peel under one particularly abused victim, its face deformed by angry welts of bubbled dough and curling anchovies. I glare at Joey. "Call it out, pendejo!" I say and heft the pizza on the peel and can't decide whether to catapult it at his face or lay it on the cutting table next to the perfect pepperoni he just sliced and shoved under the angry orange heat lamps.

Joey's frown morphs into resistance. "But, I can't—"

"The fuck can't you do?" I say. "Call the name or I swear to God, man." Dripping in the oven's heat, I choke on the smoking essence of incinerated bell peppers and crumbled linguiça so close to combustion that it glows like charcoal. I think about how I could be washing dishes at Bangkok Garden across the street. It's not as hot—and I'd get a bowl of *tom kha kai* and Thai iced tea on my break.

Joey shrugs. "If you say so, Luís." From White Joey, my name always sounds like "Louise."

"Keep it up, dickweed," I say.

He leans to the mic, flicks the button, and side-eyes me, like *See what I'm 'bout to do?*

"*JEEZ*-us, your pizza's ready! Extra-large pepperoni for *JEEZ*-us. *JEEZ*-us, come on up and get your pizza!"

Joey says *JEEZ*-us like one of those flabby-jowled TV preachers, the ones who convulse, white-knuckled, over the pulpit, armpits soaked from the faith and eyes wild with grace, amphetamines, and all the tax-deductible donations.

The crowded dining room falls silent, families frozen in wonder at the outside chance they'll get to see the real deal, one and only Son of God collect his 3,000-calorie dinner on a busy Friday night.

"You ignorant-ass *bolillo*," I say. My head spins from the smoke billowing out of the oven, but I can't bring myself to get back to work, to avert my stinging eyes, to miss the closest thing to an honest-to-God Advent I'll ever witness. "Jesús," I mumble, stepping up to the cutting counter with the burnt medium anchovy.

"What?" Joey says.

"Je-*SÚS*, bro. That's how you pronounce it."

Joey scratches his head. "Isn't that just Mexican for *JEEZ*-us?"

At the back of the dining room, next to the massive flatscreen broadcasting the Angels tied-up with the Devil Rays in the ninth, a man stands. Two hundred eyes lock onto *JEEZ*-us—Jesús—as he edges past the woman he's come with. I'd bet my entire week's minimum-wage salary that her name is María. Except this Mary is no virgin because there's an infant on her breast and a toddler on each side grinding cheap restaurant crayons into waxy crumbs that I'll have to sweep up after closing.

Jesús scans the room, a hundred expectant faces turned towards him. He musses the hair of one of the toddlers and steps around the end of the long table into the aisle that leads straight to me and Joey. He is tall, barrel chested, with a clean white button-up stretched tight over his round belly and pushed into midnight blue jeans. The sloping brim of his camel suede cowboy hat obscures his eyes, and his mouth is hidden beneath a big broom *bigote* that would make my mother blush. Polished brown boots whisper over the dense commercial carpeting, tough enough to withstand beer, grease, cigarette ash, blood, vomit, and the mortal sin of boxed wine. His thumbs are locked into a leather belt embossed with eagles clutching serpents in talon and beak. And perched over his crotch, a curved pewter buckle that shouts *¡100% Chihuahuense!* under each fluorescent light that he passes.

Joey blinks wide-eyed at his approach. "What's happening?" he whispers.

"Shut up," I say. Behind us, a ruddy flicker that might be the blinking Orange Crush sign at the bar or the first tongues of flame from the oven. I catch a whiff of brimstone—or maybe it's just ignited pizza dough. I don't care anymore.

"But—" Joey starts to say and is cowed into silence when the steel caps of Jesús's boot heels click on the tiles in front of the pick-up counter.

He flicks the brim of his hat and smiles at the extra-large pepperoni set out before him. His broad white teeth remind me of my own, teeth my welfare insurance orthodontist once called "Indian teeth" before complaining to his assistant that he should charge my mother more for the extra hardware it would take to wrestle them half-way straight.

"Esto es para usted," I croak and nudge the platter towards him.

"Muchas gracias, jovenazo," he says. Strong, calloused hands lift the aluminum platter. Laborer's hands. The hands of a *carpintero*.

"¿S-Señor?" I stutter. It occurs to me, with the clarity of a ringing bell, that *Señor* also means *Lord*.

Jesús pauses. The steam rising from the pizza hazes his face like incense smoke. "¿Mande?"

His smile is peace, his voice love. Dark pools of millennia-old eyes pull me in.

"¿En qué puedo servirle, mi hijo?" he says.

5
A PURPOSE TO OUR SAVAGERY

"Move it, Daniel."

The boy hurries to match his father's long, lanky stride. When he has caught up, he lets his eyes drift upward. Sequoias tower above them. He is awestruck by the trees' height, the deep red of their furrowed bark contrasting with spiky emerald needles. Anticipation makes him short of breath.

These woods are perfect, he thinks. For *them*.

Daniel was eager to start the hike and so didn't ask about food at the campsite. His father does have beef jerky, though, and even gives him some when the six year-old can go long enough without talking.

They walk in silence until Daniel can no longer stand it. "When will we see wolves?" he asks.

"No wolves up here. Not for over a century," his father says without turning around. "All killed off." The man's voice is deep and feels wrong out here in the woods.

Crying would ruin everything, so Daniel squints until he smashes trees and man into watery slits. He loves wolves. He knows them from the web documentaries he's spent the summer memorizing while his mother is at work. They're not like the neighborhood dogs back home, the ones that wander the vacant lots and make you wish the next bus would hurry up and come and you can watch them fight at the bus stop as they shrink to nothing in the distance.

Wolves are way better than dogs, Daniel knows, dragging his sleeve across his eyes. They have more important things to do than stalk boys on their way home from the playground. The shows say there's never been a documented human fatality from wolves in North America. For all their ferocity, Daniel understands, they have a code, a purpose to their savagery.

In his boyish narcissism, where the earnestness of his longing is a virtue, it is inconceivable that the wolves would not come. They're out there, Daniel knows, regarding him, waiting for the right moment.

He watches for them through the trees.

*　*　*

Daniel looked forward to exploring the woods with his father, but now they come upon two tall, bare-legged women on the trail. He watches his father transform into something he has never seen before. Cold blue eyes become soft and hard lips stretch into an easy, lupine grin. The women throw their heads back to laugh, ponytails swinging. Their smooth, muscular necks embarrass Daniel more than their legs. His nostrils flare. They smell like sweat, cigarettes, and flowers.

He looks down and scrapes at the trail with the toe of his sneaker.

"Go back and wait at the van," his father says before heading off with the women.

Daniel stands silently in the shadow of the sequoias until their voices fade and the only sound is the breeze in the high branches. Eyes closed, he leans forward slightly and listens under the wind for other sounds that would assure him he is not alone, that he shares this space beneath the trees with something larger and more important than himself.

Something worth considering.

The trail weaves between the gargantuan sequoias. Daniel pauses at several forks in the path and is relieved that he sometimes drags his feet. Every now and then, he is convinced he sees paw prints in the rust-colored pine duff, next to his. He feels foolish that he had been looking ahead for them. They would have shadowed them from behind.

Downwind. That's how wolves do it.

He guesses correctly enough times and makes it back to the campground. Parked next to the van is a car covered in a thin patina of road dust. Daniel walks to the driver's door and tries the handle. The door creaks open and he peers inside. Plastic bags stuffed with clothes, fast food wrappers, and two bedrolls. Chin raised, he takes in the scent. Sweat, cigarettes, and flowers.

He swings the door shut and sways on his feet, dizzy enough to have to hold himself up against the car. It occurs to Daniel that he's thirsty. The van is locked, but there is a dripping water pipe jutting from the bare dirt in the middle of the campground. A yellow jacket stings him on the finger when he crouches to drink.

The day his father moved out, his mother told him that no matter what you've done or haven't done, sometimes you deserve the bad things that happen.

Daniel sits against the van squeezing his finger. Occasionally he scans the campground. Still, they do not come. He lets himself cry.

Wolves can be sad, he tells himself.

* * *

That night, Daniel lies on the ground outside the van scratching his swollen finger. He was supposed to sleep under the trees with his father, in sleeping bags, but the tall, bare-legged women stayed. Above him, stars wink through the tree branches. Each time his eyelids grow heavy, a bump, voice, or some other noise jumps from the van and chases the sleep away. Daniel knows he can't be inside the van right now. He's glad that the night smells good and that it's not raining.

But he wouldn't mind some snow. Wolves love snow.

Daniel lifts his head and stares into the blackness. The only details he can make out are the spaces above where the black sequoias give way to the spray of stars beyond. From inside his sleeping bag he pulls out a large chrome flashlight, secreted from the van. The sequoias rise straight and stolid in the torch beam, each one extending upward until it fades into the sky.

A noise brings the beam racing back to the forest floor. Daniel jerks upright and sweeps the flashlight back and forth. A rustle on the right, a shaking branch to the left. He scoots backward until he is pressed up against the van. Daniel jabs the light between the trees for the telltale sign of glowing eyes, his finger throbbing as he clutches the flashlight.

He knows better than to howl just now, so he pushes breath through moving lips. Please come, he mouths. Please come. *Please...*

A boot nudges him awake.

"Damn it, kid. You killed the batteries," says the father, flicking the flashlight switch for emphasis. Daniel blinks and sits up. One of the women is standing near the dust-covered car, working deodorant into her armpits. The other sits cross-legged in the opening of the van's side doors, yawning and running her fingernails over the soft insides of her thighs.

"Get up," his father says. "We're going down to the river."

Daniel sulks behind them, rubbing his finger against his pant leg, down down down to the river where the trees thin out and the High Sierra sun shouts off eroded granite boulders. His father tells him to stay put and goes with the women around a bend, clambering over large rocks until they're out of sight. Daniel does boy things at the river's edge, at one point falling into the water. He manages to catch hold of a dead branch before he's pulled downstream. He remembers from the documentaries how deer will sometimes run into rivers to avoid wolves. They must be very afraid to do that, he reasons, as he catches his breath on the riverbank.

Daniel scowls and puffs out his chest. I wouldn't jump in the river, he thinks, shivering. I would fight.

He's mostly dry again when hunger and boredom drive him to start searching. He considers giving up at a particularly tall piling of boulders that rises twice his height. Granite scratches his palms as he climbs. From the top, Daniel sees them. He fears that he has seen grown-up things. He knows he probably has.

Daniel thinks involuntarily of his mother and runs.

* * *

This time, he made sure to pay attention to the trail. Anger drives him up up up the mountain. With every footfall he feels stronger, more desperate. With that desperation comes a nameless purpose. His breathing, sharp bites of air, signal a newness that terrifies and thrills him. He senses them on all sides now, cunning, unseen companions bounding with him up the trail in pursuit of something invisible, just out of reach. His finger no longer hurts and his ears ring in anger and anticipation.

At the water pipe, Daniel crushes every yellow jacket he can catch with his bare hands. Several manage to sting him before they die. When his blood cools, the sight of their yellow and black bodies, smashed and scattered in the mud, floods his chest with guilty rage.

There was no purpose to this savagery, he knows. I deserve this.

Daniel's hands swell as he stalks the campground, waiting for them to come.

* * *

"Why the hell didn't you stay put?" his father roars when he and the two women return from the river. "I've been looking all over for you." The man's voice booms between the massive trunks of the sequoias.

Daniel looks down and kicks at the dirt. He clenches his swollen fists as best he can and imagines claws bursting from his throbbing fingertips. The women stand behind the man and glance at one another nervously.

"I'm talking to you," his father says and steps closer.

Daniel's stomach growls.

The father takes him by the shoulders and shakes. Daniel's head jerks back and forth before he's flung backward. They lock eyes. Daniel knows that worse is coming. Worse has happened before.

This time, he thinks that maybe his mother was wrong, that maybe sometimes you don't deserve the bad things.

Daniel closes his eyes and waits. Blades of sunlight cut angled slices through the tree shadows. The campground's dark, silty air begins to vibrate with the thrum of paws, black and gray shadows thrashing through the trees and low brush, muzzles panting. Arms raised, Daniel turns in a circle to greet them.

A howl fills the empty spaces between the trees.

He did not expect them to come like this, but he's thankful they have. This is going to happen. Wolves were made for this.

The amber-eyed alpha lowers its head, fur bristling and lips pulled back to reveal yellowed fangs. Daniel's father freezes and the women begin to retreat toward their car.

We are alone, Daniel knows. There is no one here to help us. We will break your knuckles on our heads. We will bite off your fingers. We will do what we must because there is a purpose to our savagery.

We will not win, but you will not beat us.

6
HUITZILIN

S unlight pools, trickles, and then pours over the edge of the
mesa. No sooner am I reborn than I am drawn to it, as I
am drawn to the flowers that grow in my father's yard. Sun and
nectar, *Tonatiuh* and *xochinecutli*, both in their own ways fuel
for the returned warriors, we who have been summoned to face
our private shames before we are called to fight. In the kitchen
window, my reflection, an orange spark and wings that flash
like the flint knives of our ancestors, the obsidian blades that
opened veins of eternal life onto the tongue of the Sun Stone.

Tonatiuh

You heave Yourself off of the mesa and take flight, Your
golden river now a whirlpool of fire. The universe bends under
Your weight, leans into You, falls upward...

no, por favor, todavía no

Not yet.

Beneath me, my father's prized red valerian, the only thing
that would grow in the sour soil beneath the kitchen window. I
dip to drink, its delicate blossoms the shade of my mother's too-
bright lipstick that she would wear even when gardening.

Twist, bend, attack, retreat—every flower an invitation to violence or love, my blurred wings fed by their essence.

Tonatiuh kisses my black beak. My eyes flutter with His call.

Not yet. Please.

I am distracted by a flash. A rival. Another warrior called back. We spin and joust. Our kissing shrieks bounce off the glass. She is strong—but I am home, if only for a moment.

My home. My heart. I am compelled by an undeniable need to set things right.

She retreats to a high branch of the massive honey locust that my father would call *ese pinche arbol de mierda* for all the leaves it would drop, impossible to clean, our rakes useless in the high-desert autumn. But now it is full and green—a perfect redoubt for my rival.

Through the window, I can see clearly into our kitchen. The large jar of *agua de jamaica* cooling on the table means it's Saturday.

I spin to glare at my rival. *I am home* I shout.

No time! she chirps from her perch. *He is rising!*

no, todavia no

Next to the wall phone is the calendar from the *panadería,* a new one every year, every month a new version of voluptuous Aztec maidens swooning in the arms of muscled princes, their feathered regalia bristling against a backdrop of misty mountains and glowing stepped pyramids.

Different year, same sexism, I would tease Papi.

He would just shrug and aim that sly grin of his. *No se queja tu mamá.* Your mamá doesn't complain.

Every thought of Papi threatens to calm my wings, to let myself be driven down by the regret. Only *Tonatiuh* lifts me and drives me to my last task before I go to fight forever.

I never said goodbye.

July. The calendar says July. A square in the middle of the month is circled in red pen. I press as close to the window as I dare, my feathers brushing the glass.

July 16. The year...

My wings falter, even the towering Sun can no longer hold me up. I fall into the red valerian, cradled in its velvety leaves. My rival chirps.

Four years. Of course.

* * *

M'ija, did I ever tell you about Huitzilopochli? Papi said once, towards the end. He tottered in the kitchen, holding himself up with a stick-thin arm against the sink. He was so sick.

No, Papi. You never mentioned Wee-tsee-lo-whatever, I said. Is it possible to remember what an eye roll feels like?

Pues, mira. He was the Lord Chuparrosa, the Hummingbird of the South, Tonatiuh himself.

¿A mi qué? What's it to me? I said. I couldn't look at him. Those sunken cheeks and sagging eyes. I couldn't decide which frightened me more: what the chemo did to him, or his defiant grins on the days he felt the worst.

It's just...I'm trying to teach you. When we leave this world, he waits. He is patient. Your abuelita taught me that He waits exactly four years to the day and then brings us back, as warriors, to help him. Since the beginning He honors us as huitzilin, as hummingbirds, the most furious and truthful of birds.

Why are you saying these things? I screamed, terrified and ashamed of his madness.

Because m'ija, I want you to know that I'll be back, for a little bit, after I'm gone. He gives us one chance to say goodbye before we go to war, the real war, the battle He fights every night to be able to return to us in the morning. He only chooses the strongest. Papi smiled at me, the pride bringing a temporary flicker to his hollow eyes. *Only His chosen ones are allowed to make things right a last time before they serve Him.*

You can't seriously believe that superstitious Indian shit! I said. I railed at him. I hated him for being sick, for making me miss him before he was gone, for trying so hard—and now for going insane. I ran. I ran to the garage and slammed the car door before he could catch me, frail from the radiation. I watched him shrink in the rearview and gasped through the tears when he fell, sprawling on the pavement.

* * *

A whirring nearby, past the blossoms. *He calls. Get up!* My rival's wings stir the leaves above me.

I rise. *Tonatiuh-Huitzilopochtli,* the Sun, bounces from my feathers, blood-orange jewels dazzle in the window's reflection.

My rival, my companion, *no coayotl*, retreats again to her branch. *Hurry!* she chirps.

I know she is right. With every minute, the roar of *Tonatiuh's* fire is louder, morem irresistible, more perfect. A shadow in the hallway, beyond the kitchen. I throw myself at the window.

No coayotl, my companion, screams from her branch.

Again, I crash into the window.

Tonatiuh-Huitzilopochtli's rays make music only my soul can hear. *You are of no use to me broken, little one,* He says.

I dash myself against the glass a third time. Movement in the hallway now. Papi totters into the kitchen, that bemused look on his face that always made me giggle. He is bent, but his cheeks are full, his eyes open and alert.

Alive. My Papi is alive.

I turn to let the Sun dance off of my feathered armor. I lift my sword-like beak and whoop. My companion responds from her branch. A shared war cry.

Papi smiles vaguely and then steps to the table. He wraps his hands around the glass jar, testing the *agua de jamaica*.

I spin and whirl, throw my most furious poses, but he does not notice. My warrior blood froths at the snub. *I am HOME!* I shout. *I am HERE!*

Papi lifts the jar and starts to turn away.

I speed at the window, heedless of my tiny body or my companion or *Tonatiuh* or the coming battle. The glass cracks and I tumble, crashing through the branches of the red valerian until I fall through to the dirt below. From the honey locust, panicked chirps. Towering *Tonatiuh-Huitzilopochli* groans, his light unable to reach me under the bush.

* * *

I lie beneath the valerian and let myself remember the end of a different life, a wasted life, a life of weakness and fear. The car a twisted shell around my broken body. Papi pulling uselessly at the door. *Come back to me, m'ija! Come back to me!* I remember the papery scrapes of his irradiated voice, the dazzling sunlight through the shattered windshield fading to black...

* * *

I try to stand and lurch sideways. My leg is broken, but my obsidian wings are still keen. They lift me again and the Sun's call is stronger than ever. My companion's shrieks are blood-thirsty and feral. She is close to giving in.

no, todavia no

Papi peers wide-eyed through the window, his face haloed

by the spiderweb crack I have left in the glass. I rise before him. My broken leg hangs low, but my armor glows fierce in the light. I bob, I weave, I thrust and parry for him. *I am HERE!* I bellow. *I am STRONG!*

I hover in the chill morning fire and then approach the window. I stare into my father's clouded, brown eyes. *I am SORRY!*

Papi jerks back, trips against the table. The jar of *agua de jamaica* falls and shatters at his feet spraying crimson hibiscus across the floor. Slowly, he turns his head, eyes locked onto me until he faces the wall. He stares at the calendar and then turns back to the window, eyes sparkling, proud tears scarring his cheeks.

Behind me a rush of wind. *No coayotl* hovers. Her beak flashes in the Sun. *It is time. We must go to Him.* Her chirps are savage challenges to any who would resist.

She is right.

Tonatiuh-Huitzilopochli floods all with His light. *Come, Little Ones, my furious yaotiacahuan. My precious jade warriors. Take your place among us,* He sings.

I lower my beak and gently, carefully, press my orange head against the window. Papi lifts his trembling palm to the glass. For a moment we are still, the only movement my blurring wings.

I love you, I chirp and pull back. The Sun...

It calls. If this was my penance, my duty, then the coming war is my reward. Like an arrow, my companion lances skyward, no longer able to resist the call. She becomes a tiny dot against *Tonatiuh-Huitzilopochli's* golden face.

I rise into the light and glance down, one last time. Papi stands on the back porch now, his robe flapping against his skinny legs in the morning breeze. Through his tears, he yells, fists raised in the air. His face radiates love. I toss my head back and let loose a cry that would make eagles cower—regret, guilt, anger, shame, but also pride, courage, redemption. I point myself at the Sun. I race upward to the only war that was ever worth fighting.

Above the roar, Papi's last shout comes through. *Go, m'ija.*

And so I become light.

7

A PLACE TO CALL HOME

"**S** ssso, explain to us, young man, why you believe we should proceed with thisss transaction?"

The strange voice had introduced itself as Mr. Dessousmer.

Ricky pressed the phone against his ear and glanced down at himself. His shirtsleeve had ridden up to reveal angry red lines crisscrossing the underside of his skinny forearm. "Um, Mr. Dessousmer," he said, "when I saw the link to your web page, what you're advertising—I knew I'd be right for them. They're interesting."

Interesting enough to follow the website's instructions. No online forms. No emails. No texts. You actually had to *call the number and speak to someone*. Who even does that anymore? he wondered.

But for this, Ricky knew, he would have done almost anything.

"Indeed, young man. Interesting isss one word for them." Mr. Dessousmer's voice curled into Ricky's ear like ink through water. "But interest alone isss insufficient," the voice continued.

"There must be a *reason* for said interest? A compelling need, *hmm?*"

Ricky closed his eyes and breathed deeply. This is too weird, he thought. I should just hang up.

But there was something in the voice, something inexplicably sincere, that made him want this all the more. Ricky swayed rhythmically on his bed, phone mashed to the side of his head. "I just know they would be perfect for me," he said, "and me for them."

* * *

On the porch was a small box with no postage or obvious markings other than a blue logo featuring a swirl of lines, waves maybe, circling a handsome eyelike symbol. The same symbol as on the website.

Ricky frowned and looked up and down the street. It had only been a day since he spoke with Mr. Dessousmer.

The box was light and made no sound when Ricky shook it gently. He keyed in and walked briskly down the hallway, past his parents' master and Connor's room. Along the way, his eyes passed over the family photos lining the wall: Connor's Eagle Scout ceremony, Connor's eighth-grade graduation, and Connor's letterman banquet. Ricky paused at the only one including himself: Cabo San Lucas three summers ago, to celebrate Connor's entry to high school. The four of them stood on the beach; Connor, tall and handsome, had his arm around his mother, Linda. Ricky's father beamed at the camera, hand resting on Connor's shoulder. And in the back stood Ricky, pale and hunched behind Connor, two years younger and a full head shorter than his stepbrother.

He hurried the rest of the way to his room at the end of the hallway, box tucked tightly under his arm. He placed the box on the bed and kneeled down to admire it. The perfect, platonic ideal of a box. No dents, crushed corners, or smudges, the cardboard tape so expertly spread over the container's seams that it might as well have been skin. Ricky ran his fingers over it, tracing a line in the tape with his fingernail.

Without thinking, he reached into the nightstand next to the bed and removed a razor blade. Halfway to the soft, white underside of his forearm, the blade stopped. Ricky brought the razor to eye level. On its edge was a dull, brownish smear where, on the bad days, he would lay it flat and push the blood across his arm.

But not today. Maybe not ever again, Ricky thought, pulling his sleeves down to his wrists.

He exhaled and slowly ran the blade over the brown paper tape. It parted with a clean, dry hiss that made his pulse quicken.

When he was done, he returned the razor to the nightstand and slowly, carefully opened the lid.

* * *

"Brine shrimp," Mr. Dessousmer said. He laughed, a moist, gurgling sound that reminded Ricky of blowing bubbles in the bath water when he was little. "*Artemia*. Aqua Dragonsss," the voice went on. "The medieval Persians called them 'water dogs.' Alas, they are simply brine shrimp."

"The magazine ad called them Sea-Monkeys. I tried to take care of them, but they died after a day."

"Indeed," said Mr. Dessousmer. Ricky thought that maybe he heard regret. "Cryptobiosis—the eggs remain in stasis until one providesss the right conditions, but then they die, deprived of nutrients. They live and yet are wholly inadequate for your purpose. An unfortunate waste of life—if one can call an existence free of companionship a life." Mr. Dessousmer paused, as if waiting for Ricky to respond. "It wasss not your fault," the voice said, finally. "You could not have known."

Ricky felt the tension in his chest release, like a tendon being cut. It was not his fault.

"Will you send them to me?" he asked, glancing at his laptop for the hundredth time.

Companions: Feeling Alone? Grow Your Own!
Caretaker consultations by phone only.

"We are as of yet undecided," the voice said. "A few more questionsss, if you please."

* * *

Inside the box were two oblong capsules, each roughly the size of Ricky's thumb.

The capsules were snugly embedded, side-by-side, in a greenish foam that gave off a rich, fecund odor. Ricky thought it smelled like dried seaweed. He ran a finger over one of them. Its surface was soft, yet sturdy, and gave only slightly beneath his touch. Ricky's eyelids fluttered, his mind caressed by ocean sounds—the rhythm of surf, frothing sea mist, the sizzle of breakers receding from a sandy beach. And deeper rumblings, the groans and clicking of massive things that moved slowly and sang for eons, never alone in the dark. Awash in the sounds, Ricky felt no need for words, those clumsy tools that had never fully conveyed his deepest thoughts.

The front door slammed. Ricky fell onto the floor.

"You home, dickweed?" Connor yelled from down the hall.

Ricky scrambled to his knees and shoved the box under his bed.

* * *

"I have a terrarium that I can fill with water, and my own room, and a closet that I can keep dark," Ricky said, wincing into the phone. The still-raw cuts burned beneath his shirtsleeve.

"Very good, young man," Mr. Dessousmer purred. "We have no doubt you would provide the material necessities, but more about *you*. We must be sure that we—the companionsss, rather—are placed with those who will value them most. Those with whom they can establish a...*rapport*."

"I will be there for them, Mr. Dessousmer. I promise."

"Why doesn't a sensitive young man like yourself just start with a dog?"

"My parents won't let me have one," Ricky said quietly. "Too messy." With every slithering word from Mr. Dessousmer, Ricky felt his squirming emotions evening out, settling deeper into a quiet, calm space that helped to order his mind. "They're okay with fish, though, or anything I can keep in my tank." He sighed. "I'm tired of lizards."

Ricky closed his eyes and waited for a response. He felt more than heard what came through the phone—a low, rumbling vibration that slipped into the silent spaces behind his conscious thoughts. The soft presence browsed through his drifting memories, not so much an intrusion, but bearing witness: the darkened hospital room; the smothering, antiseptic air; the wires and tubes connecting his mother to the phalanx of murmuring machines next to her bed. Ricky's eyes began to glaze over. "Hello?" he forced himself to say.

"Yes," the voice answered. "We have decided that you would be a suitable recipient. Our first, in fact. Congratulationsss."

Ricky's mouth fell open. "But," he said, his vision beginning to clear, "there's no price on your web page." He had scanned the site so many times, committed every word to memory, but nowhere did it say how much they would cost. Just a blurry, almost abstract image of two vaguely human figures, floating side-by-side, the silhouettes of their heads punctuated by two swirling eyes.

"That is of no concern. Consider this a trial, a way for usss to test the market, so to speak." Mr. Dessousmer's words were accented with a delicate hiss that made Ricky's eyelids heavy. "What is most important to usss is a suitable intimate. A good fit, you might say."

"I can be that," Ricky said, barely above a whisper.

Again, the gurgling laugh. "Good! But with this agreement comes responsibilities. You will not be their owner sso much as their *partner*. Based on just this interaction, we are confident you will bond."

"Bond?" Ricky said.

"Indeed. Imprint. Now, let usss discuss what you must do once they arrive."

* * *

Ricky stood at the kitchen counter, silently reciting Mr. Dessousmer's steps for incubating the capsules.

The microwave rang out its happy, inane ding.

He opened his eyes. Connor's chiseled, angular face hovered before him. Deep blue eyes searched Ricky's before narrowing into slits.

"God, you really need to get *this* shit"—Connor gestured at all of Ricky— "fixed if you're ever going to get any girls to talk to you at school. Fucking hopeless, dude." He opened the microwave and ran his finger over the dripping remains of exploded Hot Pockets. "Make me some more," he said. "This time, one minute. Can't you follow instructions? I wish Mom and your dad had taken you with them on vacation and not dumped you with me."

Ricky imagined kneeing Connor in the junk, spitting on his writhing body, and dumping the kitchen table over him for the *grand finale.* The fantasy collapsed under the weight of what he knew would really happen: Connor would deftly avoid the knee with some ninja-like move, bustle Ricky into the bathroom, and shove his head deep into the toilet. Another doomed attempt at cosmic justice ending in a bloody-nosed swirlie.

Connor looked Ricky up and down. "Just make sure you're out of the way tonight. Sandra's coming over."

"Dad and Linda said no girlfriends or parties," Ricky said as he rinsed the obliterated Hot Pockets off of the microwave dish. He sighed in frustration at the sink sprayer's weak stream. The longer it took him to finish this, the longer he had to be around Connor.

"Sandra's not a girlfriend, she's a *classmate.* And we won't be partying, we'll be *stu-dy-ing,*" Connor said with a thrust of his hips on each syllable. The thrusts stopped when he noticed Ricky's forearm. "What the f—"

Ricky pulled his sleeves down and tossed two more pastries into the microwave.

"Just..." Connor said, his expression a mix of revulsion and what Ricky thought might be fear. "Just stay the hell out of the way, and none of your Harry Potter or gamer nerd bullshit while she's here. Got it? Sandra's hot."

And really, really nice, Ricky thought. One of the only kids willing to say hi to me at school. With a start, he remembered the box under his bed. "I'll need to use the bathroom tub tonight," he said, punching one minute into the oven keypad.

"Do not *even* tell me you're gonna take a bubble bath while Sandra's here."

"It's for a science project, for school." Ricky knew the best way to get Connor to lose interest would be to use the words *science* and *school* in the same sentence.

Connor aimed a finger at Ricky's face. "Whatever, dweeb. Like I said, no geek shit and do not even think about getting near my room tonight."

*　*　*

Ricky slid the box from under his bed and set it on his lap. Music from Connor's room thumped through the walls. With his thumb and forefinger, Ricky gently lifted the capsules from the pungent foam and raised them to the light on his nightstand. Inside, each one glowed a milky aquamarine. He turned them slowly but couldn't make out anything more substantial than an indistinct denseness in the middle of each.

"Warmth iss good," Mr. Dessousmer had said. "You may use a lamp, but your palms would be preferable. For the imprint."

Ricky sat on the floor, his back against the bed, and closed his fingers around the capsules. He had already set the water heater to maximum in the garage and would need to start the tub soon.

Before long, he felt a warmth in the center of each palm spreading up to his wrists. The cuts on his left forearm stung and then calmed as the heat crept toward his shoulders and chest. When it reached Ricky's neck, his head lolled backward onto the mattress. Ricky forced his eyes open, but what he saw was no longer entirely his bedroom. Thick stalks of kelp swayed in formation, bending upward through slanting blades of green sunlight that shone through his window. Creatures flitted through their leaves, perfectly in tune with their purpose in the world. Singly and in groups, the fishes and otters and turtles

54

swam to a rhythm that made them part of something larger and more meaningful than themselves.

With an ache in his chest, Ricky knew that none of these creatures were ever truly alone.

His heartbeat slowed, keeping time with an order and calmness he had never known. Beyond the kelp, he caught glimpses of something utterly new, neither fish, nor otter, nor turtle. Something unexpected yet totally natural. They drifted through the kelp grove, almost playfully. Desire exploded in Ricky's chest, a longing so intense it seemed he might turn himself inside out. Inch by inch, they came closer, obscured by the dense growth. Ricky rolled his head to the side and found himself face to face with one of them.

Its eyes—

The doorbell rang.

Disoriented, Ricky rolled to his knees, the capsules still cupped in his palms. His room was dark and night had fallen outside his window. How long have I been here? he wondered. The clock on his nightstand read almost nine. Past his door, the sounds of Connor stepping quickly down the hallway. Ricky placed the capsules under his pillow and stumbled to his feet.

Again, Mr. Dessousmer's voice floated in his mind. "Once you have prepared them, it isss time to run the water. Hot enough to cause sssome discomfort, but not to burn."

Ricky stepped into the hallway and made his way toward the kitchen where Sandra was leaning against the counter.

"Hey, bud," Connor said, his words clipped. "Didn't realize you'd be out here."

"Hi, Ricky." Sandra smiled. Ricky stood for a moment to admire her red hair and lilting voice, always so upbeat. "Connor said you'd be using the tub tonight," she said. "Something about an experiment for school."

Connor crossed the kitchen and threw a muscular arm over

Ricky's shoulders. "Oh yeah, Ricky's got a project he's working on. Kinda the family genius, aren't ya?" he said, his arm tightening around Ricky's neck. "His mom would be proud of him. Wouldn't she, Ricky?"

Ricky craned his neck to look into Connor's miles-deep blue eyes, his smile showcasing perfectly straight teeth.

"I...yeah," Ricky stammered. "Hi. Sandra." The three stared at one another until Ricky twisted away from Connor. "I have to get something from the garage," he croaked and flung himself out the door. Outside, he leaned against the wall, his hands balled into fists.

Never had Connor mentioned his mother before.

"I feel bad for him, Con. He's always by himself at school," he heard Sandra say through the door.

"Don't worry about it. I watch out for him," Connor said. "That's what big brothers are for, right?"

Ricky stepped off the landing, unable to listen anymore. Next to the water heater, he found a thirty-pound bag of salt pellets. "You will need approximately two pounds of sssalt," Mr. Dessousmer had said. He hefted the bag and waddled back up the steps into the kitchen.

"Wow, Ricky! I don't remember having to do anything so serious for freshman science lab!" Sandra laughed. Ricky tripped against the kitchen table. "Help him, Con," she said. "That bag looks heavy."

Connor glared at Ricky. "No prob," he said. "Let's get that to the bathroom, champ." Connor took a corner of the salt bag, and together they walked it down the hallway. At the bathroom door, Connor stole a glance toward the kitchen and leaned into Ricky, their foreheads touching. "Listen, you little nutsack," he growled. "This is the last I want to see you tonight. Stay the fuck outta sight or I'll make you wish you were in the car with your psycho mom when she went over the edge."

* * *

"You said I'd be the first. Why me, Mr. Dessousmer?"

"Why indeed, young man," the voice whispered. "Unlike the sso-called *Sea-Monkeys* you naively attempted to raise, your new companions will be quite sensitive to you—your moods, needs, desires—particularly early in the hatching process. They mustn't be ignored, and we are quite confident that you have the temperament and motivation to best care for them. They mussst receive your undivided attention."

Ricky closed his eyes and pressed the phone harder against his ear. "I understand, Mr. Dessousmer. I won't let you down."

* * *

He turned the hot water on full and hurried back to his room. The underside of his pillow was warm, and the odor rising from the capsules reminded him of the sushi his family had ordered to celebrate Connor's first place at State in the 182-pound class. He listened for a moment at his stepbrother's door. Ricky heard a muffled laugh from Sandra and had to fight down a wave of resentment. Sandra could get anyone, Ricky thought. Why *him*?

The tub was half-full now. Ricky tested the water with his fingers, then turned off the faucet. "Perfect," he said, carefully lowering the capsules into the water. They floated for a few seconds before slowly sinking to the bottom of the tub.

Ricky ripped open the bag of salt.

"About two poundsss," Mr. Dessousmer had told him. "More than that would be...counterproductive. Much more...disastrous." Ricky vaguely remembered something about "uncontrolled growth...excessive hunger..."

Ricky grunted as he lifted the heavy bag over the edge of

the tub. The pellets began to plop into the water, each one spiraling downward to join the rest covering the dark green capsules.

The pile of salt moved. No, I'm imagining it, Ricky thought.

On the other side of the bathroom wall, voices and a bump from Connor's bedroom. Wait, definite movement from beneath the pile. Ricky jerked away in surprise, and the bag slipped from his wet hands. His mouth opened in a silent scream at the sight of thirty pounds of salt pellets tumbling into the tub.

"Oh fuck, oh fuck, oh fuck," he gasped. Panic drove his hands into the steaming water to save the capsules. Just as quickly, he stopped himself for fear of damaging them. He tried scooping up the salt pellets and groaned when they dissolved in his fingers.

Think, think, think, idiot. Water. Dilute the salt with more water.

Ricky turned on the faucet and yanked the shower curtains shut. The irrational idea of Mr. Dessousmer knowing what had happened filled him with shame. He chose me! Ricky thought. Me!

A moan came through the wall, barely audible over the rush of water into the tub.

The terrarium! Ricky jumped up and ran to his bedroom. In the closet, he found the five-gallon tank that would be the temporary home to his new companions. His mind raced: fill it with fresh water and then some of the salt water from the tub and then fish out the capsules.

He carried the tank down the hallway, shuffling sideways to keep it from hitting the walls. Passing Connor's door, he heard voices again. Ricky slowed to listen, but a splash from the tub sent him waddling to the kitchen sink to fill the tank with the sprayer. "Hurry, hurry, *hurry* you piece of shit!" he whimpered, furious at the sprayer's lack of urgency.

Adrenaline allowed him to carry the half-filled tank back down the hallway at a gallop. A dark crescent of water had begun to creep onto the carpet in front of the bathroom. He turned the corner to face the tub and gasped.

The tank shattered against the tile floor.

* * *

"There may be sssome...*disorientation*...at first, as they seek you out, reach out to you."

Ricky's head spun. "What am I supposed to do then? How will I take care of them?"

"Ah, young man, it will be challenging, but it isss also wondrous. I will not cheapen the experience with details, but you should know that your mind, your consciousness, will not be entirely your own in their presence. They will share themselves with you, and you with them, until it isss time for their release."

"*Release?* You mean I won't be able to keep them?" Ricky sat heavily on the bed. Eyes stinging, his fingertips sought out the still-raw cuts on his left forearm. He pressed hard with his thumb.

"Correct. We see that you are calling from a coastal city. Is that right?"

Ricky frowned, confused. "Uh-huh, Capitola." He looked out his bedroom window. The hazy blue line of the Pacific was visible just above the neighbor's house.

"And you are near the sssea?" Mr. Dessousmer asked. At the word *sea*, his silken voice took on a reverential quality.

"Yes," Ricky said. "Just a couple blocks."

"Brilliant. You will be their caretaker," Mr. Dessousmer

said, his voice soothing and even, "and they your wards, your companionsss. You will learn from one another. But, like all good relationsships, it will evolve, *they* will evolve. At a certain stage of development, before they grow too large, you will need to return them to the sssea."

"How will I know when I have to set them free?"

"They will make you aware," Mr. Dessousmer said. "When you have done this, we may discuss another delivery."

"Another delivery?" Ricky said. "You mean I could have more? To grow and take care of?"

"Perhapsss. If things go well," said Mr. Dessousmer.

* * *

This time Ricky was certain it was Sandra's voice he heard through the wall.

Something—*two* things, he realized—stood in the tub behind the shower curtain. Each figure swayed slowly, obscured by the opaque plastic. The bathroom's humid air thrummed, a barely perceptible vibration that seemed to tickle the inside of Ricky's head, just behind his ears. His eyes rolled back as he collapsed onto the flooded bathroom floor, shards of broken tank glass biting into his shoulders and back.

Through vision not his own, Ricky was blinded by a field of milky white. He watched webbed fingers reach out to slice fine lines in the shower curtain with shining black claws. Past the torn plastic, a boy lay writhing in water stained pink with blood, the entire scene distorted and curved, as if Ricky looked down on himself through a fish-eye lens. Four sets of claws tore at the plastic until the curtain rod fell clanging to the floor.

Ricky rolled over to face them, his stomach lurching from the vertigo of following his every movement through their eyes. Their heads nearly touching the ceiling, they towered above him, swaying on thin legs that belied their immense strength. On their necks, horizontal flaps of skin flicked open and closed. Gills, Ricky thought distantly. The creatures' webbed hands explored the bathroom's misty air, clawed fingers sifting the water vapor. Their skin glistened a smoky gray and black, and subtle stripes bent around their torsos.

Ricky pushed himself to his knees and cried out from the glass bristling on his back. His outburst sent a shiver through the hulking creatures in the tub, and for the first time, they focused on him and him alone. Ricky's head swam under their gaze—swirling galaxies of azure and white pierced by bottomless black pupils.

Three beings experienced the world as one. Curiosity, wonder, terror, companionship—all coursed through Ricky. The boy's eyes fluttered yet again, his consciousness torn away —to the hospital room, to his mother's hand, trembling from beneath the covers.

* * *

"I'm so sorry, baby," his mother had whispered from her bed.

"It's okay."

"No." Her hand tightened around his. "It's all right to say it, Ricky. It's not fair," she said. "I wish I knew why I was like this. I wish I knew how to be happy." She pulled his hand to her cheek and kissed it. "I need you to know that it—what I tried to do—it wasn't about you. You know that, right, baby?"

Ricky nodded and laid himself across his mother's broken body, his tears wicking into the front of her thin, cotton gown. He wondered if things would have been different if, just for once, it had been about him.

"I need to know that you'll be all right," his mother whispered, combing his hair with her fingers. "I need you to look at me and tell me that you'll choose to be all right." She lifted his face and wiped his cheeks dry. "Choose, Ricky."

* * *

The creatures regarded the boy kneeling on the bathroom floor, pulled into a memory not their own, yet universal in its essence.

MOTHER

HOME

The urge resounded through his body like a church bell, a deep, resonant note vibrating from within. He stared into the eyes of the newborn creatures. Despite his terror, Ricky felt the inexorable pull of their connection, a link between the soul and the flesh that bound them to one another.

HOME!

The first companion stepped over the edge of the tub, followed immediately by the second. Ricky pushed himself into the hallway, the bottoms of his bare feet prickling as the creatures stepped onto the broken glass.

Ricky could now clearly hear noises coming from Connor's room. The first companion jerked its head toward the noise. Narrow, impossibly muscled shoulders swung about.

Frantic voices from behind the door. Moaning.

Ricky shook with a white-hot anger. "Why?" he whispered to the creatures. "Why does he get everything that he wants—*every fucking thing*—and I have nothing?" Salty tears ran into his mouth. "How come everybody loves *him?*" The creatures gazed down at him, their heads cocked. "Well, I don't!"

"Ricky!" Connor shouted. "What the hell is all the noise? Shut the fuck up or I swear I'm gonna come out there."

"I don't love him!" Ricky shrieked.

The companions stood on guard, galvanized by the boy's

rage. Their sparkling eyes flared, and the stripes on their torsos seemed to pulse in agitation.

Ricky pushed the back of his head against the wall and sobbed. "I *hate* him!"

The first creature stepped in front of the door. Two sinewy arms shot forward like pistons. Wood exploded and hinges bent.

Through eyes not his own, Ricky took in the scene beyond the door: Sandra's legs straddling Connor; his stepbrother wiggling out of his shirt; Sandra's sparkly black bra reflecting the glow from the creature's eyes.

Both turned and screamed at the monstrosity stepping through the obliterated doorway. Sandra threw herself onto the floor and crouched in a corner of the room. Connor remained wide-eyed and frozen on the bed as the companion drew closer.

Animated by Ricky's fury, its clawed hands closed like vices around Connor's head. Ricky felt more than saw his stepbrother's face pulled taut, his eyes and mouth stretched wide between glistening, pearlescent palms.

Steel-cable arms lifted Connor off the bed. His feet flailed for purchase as a desperate squeal escaped his lips.

For an instant, Ricky felt a hint of compassion—until Sandra screamed and Connor's fist thudded into the side of the companion's head.

His stepbrother's eyes widened in terror and, in a blink, disappeared.

Ricky's mouth jerked open; somehow, he tasted blood. Wet, ravenous sounds resonated inside his head and from Connor's bedroom. In his—the companion's—peripheral, Sandra threw her hands to her mouth but could not hold back the eruption of vomit through her fingers.

Ricky hauled himself to his feet and took a step toward Connor's room, but it was too late. His throat gagged on the tang of Connor's flesh, the slurried mix of bone and muscle and whatever brains his stepbrother had ever possessed. The second companion regarded Ricky passively from the bathroom doorway.

FEED

Its thin lips parted to reveal serrated teeth before it entered Connor's bedroom to join the other.

Not Sandra, Ricky mouthed, *not her, not her, not her*. One of the companions extended a long arm, slick with blood, to calm her. Sandra shrieked and heaved a thick biology textbook at the closest one.

Pain exploded across Ricky's cheek. *No! To me. Come back to me.*

The companions entered the hallway, a shred of Connor's scalp dangling from the corner of one mouth. Ricky stood up shakily and then backed toward his bedroom, followed by the creatures. Behind them, Sandra burst from the bedroom, shirt on backward and one of Connor's baseball bats in her white-knuckled hands.

The companions spun to face her.

Ricky threw up his hands. "No! Don't!"

The four of them stood silently in the hallway, waiting.

"Run," Ricky croaked. Sandra raised the bat. "No, Sandra. Run. Please," he begged.

Sandra glared at the creatures standing above her. With a pitying look at Ricky, she let the bat fall to the wet carpet and bolted for the front door.

* * *

"What we have learned is that, to thrive, we—the companionsss, rather—must bond, must find an emotional referent early in development. This requires the right kind of steward, preferably someone young, unguarded, earnest. One who has much to give, but who also has much need. Your needsss will provide purpose, the most perfect, primal expression of love. Do you understand, young man?"

Ricky blinked, disoriented, unsure whether Mr. Dessousmer's voice came from his phone or his own head.

"I—I think so," he said dreamily. His hand rose to his chest, hollow with longing. Hot tears spilled down his cheeks onto his forearm. The sting made him wince. He glanced at the nightstand drawer. "Mr. Dessousmer..."

"Yesss?" Mr. Dessousmer's voice unfurled inside him now. Ricky was almost certain words were no longer necessary, that he could simply push the thoughts out instead.

"Can I tell you something?" he whispered.

Anything, young man, Ricky heard in his head.

He licked the tears from his lips. *I'm lonely,* he thought-said. His free hand reached for the nightstand handle. From the drawer, he pulled out the razor and laid the cool steel flat against his burning arm.

We know, Mr. Dessousmer thought back.

Ricky turned the blade perpendicular. *I don't have anyone.*

We know.

The corner of the blade pushed through, just deeply enough, to begin a new statement, another line of another paragraph of a story Ricky believed should only end in more pain. He thought of his mother and the dark spells that would torture her for days or weeks, chasms of misery so deep and wide that he was certain she would never climb back out. The blade stopped its march from wrist to crook. A sob slid from his throat as he flung the razor into the drawer and slapped it shut. Blood dripped gently onto his pant leg.

I don't want to be alone anymore!

From the darkest corner of Ricky's soul, he felt it. An upwelling of hope.

WE KNOW

* * *

Ricky stumbled backward through the doorway and crashed into the nightstand. The bedside lamp wobbled and fell, painting the room in blue and black shadows. Two tall, lean silhouettes ducked carefully under the door frame after him. A pale light flickered from their swirling eyes.

The cloying aftertaste of Connor lingered on his tongue as he backed toward the closet. Ricky thought, When Dad and Mom-Linda get home... He was unable to shut out the image of them standing over the smear of what had once been Connor.

Ricky edged past the folding closet doors and pulled them shut. Through the slats, Ricky watched the two long-limbed shadows cross his room. A part of Ricky's consciousness, dissociated and distant, marveled at their languid composure, a serenity of motion that could only belong to the sea.

The fullness of Ricky's desolation pummeled him as the companions approached. With every step the creatures took, Ricky felt walls and foundations within him beginning to crumble. The excuses he had constructed to make it to the next day, and the next, and the next—every day since his mother had sent her car over the cliff—fell away. Was she thinking of him as she drove to the lookout, or when her car left the pavement and slid across the gravel, or when the tires left the ground to spin wildly in open space? Did she think of him just before the impact?

Ricky considered these questions as the companions drew closer. He reached down and squeezed his forearm hard enough to make the blood come, and he knew that nothing, no therapy or ritual of self-harm, could stave it off any longer. Watery images of what these creatures had done to Connor spilled through his mind. He deserved no better, he thought, peering through the door slats at their rippling muscles and gleaming black claws.

Take me.

Four glowing eyes blinked in comprehension. They alone could give him what he needed most. What he *deserved*.

The first stopped just beyond the closet door. A lush, living odor overwhelmed Ricky's senses. The creature's eyes shone as its awareness expanded into the closet, grasping for him.

"I said take me!" Ricky screamed.

The second drew near. Together they swayed silently, inches from him, two minds nudging themselves into the closet, absorbing, reaching, embracing Ricky's innermost need. Ricky pressed his cheek against the closet door and began to sob.

In unison, the companions began to claw gently at the flimsy wood. The doors pulled away easily, and Ricky tumbled forward into our impossibly strong arms.

"Why?" Ricky begged.

HOME, his mind hummed in response.

TAKE US HOME

* * *

Fractured moonlight glinted off the breakers, each fold of ocean slowly sharpening as it approached the beach.

High tide, Ricky thought. He glanced up to his right, to where Highway 1 cut a line across the mountainside that plunged into the sea. Under the full moon, Ricky could see the turnout where he and his mother would park to gaze at the Pacific and talk. She would act like she didn't notice his cuts and ask him about school until she fell silent. Ricky would try to keep his mother talking, but she would only tilt her head and stare out to where the sea met the sky.

One wave, larger than the rest, formed a white-tipped line that edged toward him. In its path, two dark heads bobbed, perhaps fifty yards offshore. The pair dipped beneath the rising breaker, only to reappear on the other side, four sparkling eyes seeking out Ricky.

Always on Ricky.

COME sounded in the boy's head. HOME

White froth began to curl over the breaker as it rolled closer. Ricky's bare foot made a sucking sound in the wet sand when he tried to step back.

NO, TO US

The wave broke twenty feet away, the crash raising a gust of mist that breathed over his face. Ricky planted his feet just before the water reached him. He braced for the cold but laughed when it surged past his waist. It's warm, he thought.

In the distance, the companions bobbed in the water, their attention fixed on him.

Ricky closed his eyes and waited. The surf hissed about him and hesitated, as if deciding whether to continue its march or retreat to safety.

Choose, Ricky.

He rolled onto his back and let the foaming sea lift him off his feet. Spread-eagled, his body sped with the backflow toward the bobbing shadows waiting past the next breaker. His arms flailed at the black water, and he gasped at the pale moon just before the next wave broke over him. His body tumbled and spun, heedless of up or down, air or water, sea or sky. The undertow swept him farther out, his cheeks bulging with stale air and mind beginning to vibrate.

Blind in the darkness, Ricky threw his hands outward, into the void. Bubbles erupted from his mouth. He waited for the lung panic that did not come. The vibration behind his ears grew stronger.

I am here, he sent.

WE KNOW

New sounds came to Ricky's ears, inviting him farther into the deep. On the edge of his new senses existed a world of life that waited to welcome him.

His hands searched the dark water. *Where are we going?*

Large, webbed fingers wrapped around Ricky's arms. On either side of him, glittering eyes pierced the black.

HOME

8

COME STAI, DAVID?

"**C**ome stai, David?"

I love how Beppe lowers his head after asking me how I am, every morning on my way to the Archives. His doe eyes drift downward as he sorts his magazines and newspapers. He makes such a show of acting nervous when I walk past.

As if *I* could make *him* nervous.

"Buon giorno. Va bene, Guiseppe," I said the first time we met. In that instant those eyes became deep, wide pools.

"No, no, no!" he protested, waving his hands. "Per te...*Beppe.*" For *you...Beppe.*

Beppe isn't the only one I greet on my way through the *piazza*, a block from the Palazzo Medici. There's Paula, the young woman who sells flowers a couple of stalls down. She eyes me and Beppe and then winks as I approach, her red lips sliding into a sly grin. It's gratuitous. Maybe even a little condescending.

But can I help that it puts me at ease? That she knows and I don't have to worry?

I buy flowers from Paula when I can. Not many. My fellowship only goes so far. Just enough to express my appreciation and then later give them to the archive assistants. They cluck their tongues at me and say, in the most beautifully accented English, that the pollen is bad for the manuscripts.

But thank you, they say. Mille grazie, David.

One morning I leave the apartment early, my cheeks a little flush. Beppe is just opening his stand. "Ah, David! Che sorpresa!" he gushes. I'm happy to have surprised him.

We alternate staring into one another's faces. At our own shoes. At each other's shoes.

Shoe gazing.

"Bene allora," I say after too long saying nothing. *Alright then.*

Beppe holds me for a moment with those deep Florentine eyes. *I hope you have a good day, David,* I make out from behind me as I float to Paula's stand.

"Tu sei presso bene," Paula says, shaking her head. *You got it bad.*

I roll my eyes and dig in my pocket. I pull out a wad of colorful bills I still can't decipher. "Solo una rosa, per favore."

Paula cocks her head and squints at the money. She turns to inspect her riot of flowers, still only half unpacked. Her breath catches and she leans forward, her thin, skirted waist twisting over mounds of marigolds, carnations, paperwhites, calla lilies, and zinnias. Slender fingers close on a single rose, obscenely red, its stem as long as my forearm.

She offers the rose to me and frowns at my money. "Dai, idiota," she says flatly. *Get real, dumbass.*

"Grazie, Paula," I mumble, unable to take my eyes off the rose's petals, so vulnerable yet perfect in their symmetry.

Exactly where they should be at this place and time.

Before I can talk myself out of it, I return to Beppe's stand and tap him on the shoulder.

"Per te, Beppe," I say, my throat tight.

Beppe's eyes widen, his olive skin now deathly pale. "Grazie, David," he whispers, those beautiful eyes darting to the neighboring stalls. He spins to set the rose behind the cashbox and wipes his hands nervously on his pant legs. "Va bene, c'è molto da fare oggi!" *Okay, there's a lot to do today!* Beppe turns his back, his hands a blur as he straightens the displays.

Paula watches me, hand over her mouth, when I walk quickly past her stand.

The next morning, the apartment door closes softly behind me. I stand alone in the alleyway and kill time tying my shoes, adjusting my satchel, checking my watch. I consider walking the long way around and curse myself. I take the first tentative steps toward the *piazza*.

The morning crowd is identical to yesterday, and the day before, and the day before that. Does anything ever change in Florence? I hope not.

I walk slowly, practicing my formal apology in my best Italian. I even work to copy the silky Florentine accent. Surely, Beppe would see how hard I'm trying to set things right again?

At his stall I pause and stare. There is no magazine stand. No cash box. No Beppe. Nothing. Just an open space between two other vendors who act as though nothing has ever stood in that spot since the Etruscans raced chariots through this city.

I mouth my apology as earnestly as I can and start to walk

again. As I pass the flower stand, Paula's hand comes to rest on my arm. She leans forward and looks into my face, her eyes watery.

"Come stai, David?"

9

A SEAL'S SONG

ACT I: PLAN

I t was me and Balena who came up with this.

We were forced early on to accept our limitations—orcas being fully aquatic mammals on the one flipper, and seals mostly aquatic mammals on the other—if we were to get this project on the ground, so to speak. We would need help. We would need the damn bears.

We hate the polar bears because they're idiots and eat us every chance they get. It's been that way forever. Sure, everyone accepts that Circle of Life stuff, but still, it's hard to enter into negotiations when you barely escaped last week's ice-hole ambush. Out of gratitude to Balena, I sucked it up. You know, for the greater good.

And the orcas. They eat us too and bat our dead and dying bodies through the air like some sick game of water polo. Don't let their strangeness fool you, though. They're the smartest and toughest things in the Sea. If this were a water fight, those behemoths would run the table, a frothing red tide from horizon to horizon, nothing alive that they didn't say so. Those clicks and whistles and teeth... How could the Sea conjure such flawless beasts?

Sometimes it's like their purpose is to remind the rest of us of our imperfections—or maybe give us the opportunity to be better than we are. I didn't have much to lose, even before Balena found me. Ever since I could talk, the cows called me things like petulant, disrespectful, and contrary. The other yearlings called me worse things. I admit that I can be difficult, but I was able to convince Whiskers and Balls to do this. I'm trying not to feel guilty about that.

But even those two know that this isn't about me, that it's about the fish. The orcas eat the fish and us, and the bears eat us and some fish and the occasional orca that washes up, and we eat *lots* of fish. The one thing we all have in common is the fish. Without fish, the system's off, and when the system's off, we die—whale, bear, and seal alike. Men like fish too, apparently. Every day they go out in their boats and toss out their deadly, drifting clouds and scoop up more fish than my colony could eat in a year. No matter how much I've thought it over, looked at it from different angles, I can't make what the men do right in my head.

The truce started with the nets. We and the orcas tried breaking them, but too many of us were shot from the boats or caught in the nets. Too many died. The men acted as though we were trying to steal *their* fish. The Old Bull claimed it was a plot, a part of Balena's master plan to do away with us, once and for all. I tried to convince him that without us, the orcas would suffer. Go figure that's when the fat bastard faked like he was deaf and sent me packing.

The cows say I have a special talent for getting into trouble and bringing the wrong kind of attention to myself. It's not like I'm trying to cause problems. It's just that they don't try hard enough. For them, good enough is just fine. And lately, not enough will also do. I can't accept that.

My time to prove them wrong came a half-moon ago. Just my luck that I ended up getting snagged trying to break a big, heavy net. I thrashed so hard the men decided to cut the whole thing loose. For days I fought to get my hind flipper free until that last time I came up and knew it was over. I took one last gulp of beautiful air and made my peace. The net pulled me farther down than I'd ever been before. It was dark. My lungs burned. I didn't want it, but I was ready.

That's when I heard it, the whistles and clicking. The terror we call Balena.

I'm not sure I can do her justice. When she passes above, between us and the surface, I swear it's like one of those human submarines blocking out the moon and stars, the only difference being that she actually belongs to the world and those man-whales don't. She eats *a lot*, but we've always known her to be fair. She's living proof that it's possible to be feared and loved at the same time.

That far down the water grew eerily still and my head felt thick, as though a huge set of jaws closed gently on my skull. Balena's singing rose from the nothingness. Old cows told stories of this. Balena's Dream Song. We'd always thought they just made it up to scare us pups, but it's real. By the Sea, it's real.

The old, gray cows always said that the seal who heard the Dream Song was either dead or would be soon, that only the most ancient orcas shared the Song with the prey they valued the most. They said it was an honor to be eaten at Song's end, and then they would snicker at us behind their flippers when we shivered in fear and threw our heads back to wail at the night sky.

Balena's song was the most beautiful sound I'd ever heard,

more beautiful than raindrops pattering the waves, than the wind blowing sand across a beach, more haunting even than the gulls' cries as they ride the gusting air above the colony. Balena's moans and whistles came to me from farther than the stars in the sky, stars I found that I could see clearly in the void, so divine that I almost forgot I was drowning. The Dream Song conjured the star shapes we all learned as pups: the Blue Whale, the Shark's Tail, the Gyrfalcon, the Kelp Grove, the achingly beautiful Two-headed Swan.

Then the star-points swirled into new shapes. Fish, countless numbers, schooled around me, flitting and dancing. I grinned in the blackness at the sight until, slowly, the fish-stars began to disappear, snatched away by webs of light. The webs —nets, I realized—pulled and heaved until all the fish were gone and I was left alone in the depths to sink.

No, not alone.

I opened my eyes as wide as I could, the blackness so deep it had a presence. The Dream Song became substance, as large as the Deep and as wise as the Sea. The Song changed pattern, its moans eliding into chatter that tickled my neck. She was close, close enough to touch. In the dark, a flash. Something white. Teeth. Many, many teeth.

{quite the predicament, little one}

Balena whistled at me, gently poking her jaws through the net that would be my death shroud.

{you fought well—i've been watching} she clicked.

It's a blessing and a curse that we seals can understand orca.

"Please sing again. I'm ready," I gurgled, using the last of my air. Carefully avoiding the net, she brought her great eye up to my face. Her teeth. The last thing I'd see would be her rows of perfect white teeth. All fifty-two of them. I closed my eyes.

{no, not yet}

I hardly felt it when Balena's jaws separated me from the rotting half of my flipper, the half caught in the net. Next thing I knew, she was pushing me up up up, escorted by her harem of hunter-killers. I wanted to escape, not to safety, but down, back to the Song. It hurt to have been so close and then have it taken away. Instead, I would become a plaything for their young, slowly nibbled to nothing for sport.

Screw the Circle of Life.

I awoke to the soft, uneven rhythm of lapping water. My hind flipper throbbed. I looked down and saw my own blood staining the ice where I lay, half of one flipper bitten cleanly off. A short distance away, three big polar bears eyed me, noses raised high. No doubt I smelled delicious.

A splash behind me.

Just off the edge of the ice, several orcas bobbed, occasionally rising high enough out of the water to make sure the bears knew they were there. In the middle of them, Balena's great bulk lolled and floated. She rolled an eye upward and looked at me for a long time before saying anything.

{*good, half-fin! call to the bears; call them to you*}

I frowned at the rough-looking trio of ragged bears. "I'd rather *you* eat me than them," I coughed.

{*they will not eat you; i will not let them; call to them; we need their help*}

That monster. A mix of revulsion and admiration sent a chill up my spine. "You used me as bait," I growled.

Balena bobbed high out of the water and looked straight at me. Is it even possible for orcas to smile?

* * *

I was the one who thought to use fire. The polar bears knew about it, but it was obvious that Balena and her guards had no clue. They all listened as I told them about the fishing boat I'd sunk last summer, when I was still technically a pup. I had snuck aboard at night to steal back some of the fish they'd taken and accidentally knocked over one of their fire boxes, the things men use to make light because they're so helpless in the dark. I managed to snatch one fish before slipping off the rear deck. From the water, I watched the fishermen jump overboard to escape the glowing tongues of flame, marveling at how the fire had followed the amber liquid wherever it spilled, like a seal chasing a school of sardines. The violence and heat in that yellow light was terrifying and thrilling. Even the men fled from it.

Balena came up with the rest of the plan, with me translating for the moronic bears. It seemed like a long shot, but if we could pull it off...

She charged me and the polar bears with recruiting our best and bravest. We would meet at the rocky beach east of the fishing village at the next full moon, which was only seven nights away. The bears complained that they didn't live like seals—"nose to ass," as they put it—and that it would take more time to collect the numbers necessary to destroy the village.

With a patience that came from her many years, Balena reminded the bears, again, that they would not destroy or even enter the village, but rather blockade the docks to keep the men from reaching their boats. That would allow us seals to do our work.

The bears grumbled at this. They'd dealt with men before and had ample experience with their guns. "Coward sticks," they called them. We knew of them, too. Sometimes the men came to our rookery. We would flee into the water. Not everyone would make it.

The big male bear and his companions turned to leave. "We're hungry *now*," he snarled over his rolling shoulders.

Balena and her guards rose high and blasted spray from their blowholes.

{*go, half-fin! full moon, bring your best, ones like you who know what is at stake*}

ACT II: COLONY

It wasn't so much the rejection as the laughing. The fat, vain sea cucumber actually laughed at me.

The Old Bull easily outweighed me five-to-one. His mane glowed golden in the moonlight and his teeth flashed when he spoke. Even so, it wasn't hard to look him in the eye. How could he frighten me when I had been face-to-face with Balena herself?

"And this is how Her Terribleness has rewarded you for your loyalty?" the Old Bull said while aiming his snout at my missing flipper. His luxurious mane bristled in disgust.

"This is our one chance! No more nets. We're going for the boats themselves. The orcas—Balena *herself!*—and the bears, they've agreed to do this, but they need our help." I searched his face.

"Think of the fish," I pleaded. "Think of our pups!"

The Old Bull huffed and grumbled, shaking his mane and flashing his canines. "Go back to your new queen, *stump!*" he growled, his bellow echoing across the colony. "A seal's life is hard enough without having to worry about when the orcas will convince us to swim straight into their mouths. Best to live and die as we always have—by skill and luck. Why race willingly into the jaws of the Sea?"

He lifted his face to the starry sky, imperious and dismissive. His way of saying, *We are done here.* When the Old Bull realized I was not leaving, he wrapped his jaws around my neck and dragged me into the surf. My flipper caught against jagged rock and I fought not to cry out.

"Go!" he roared. "Before I lose my patience, Stump."

I felt my missing flipper more keenly than ever. Stump. That's what they'll call me now. *Half-fin* has more dignity.

I swam half the distance to the narrow beach where the colony rested. I felt the pull, that instinct to crawl into the musky seal scrum and lose myself in the collective vibration, that buzz that told us we were home, appreciated as one of the many, a part of something larger and more important than ourselves.

It was a loving, numbing anonymity that I'd never completely rejected but that never felt totally right, either. Sure, we each had names like Harelip, Sand Flea, Snagtooth (and now Stump), but ultimately, our only value was to the colony. The only seals who rose above would be the bulls of the rock and their chosen mates, their queens, those haughty cows who lorded over the rest of us and sometimes didn't even go out to hunt for themselves.

The only way a female like me could hope to earn a shred of respect would be to live long enough to have a cove full of pups, acting flattered when bulls warred over me and then acting just as compliant when one of them came to claim his prize.

I bobbed in the water, behind me the lordly and overweening bull, ahead the roiling mass of the colony. The familiar sounds of home came to me over the gentle waves. Chuffing, barks, growls, snores. Within that mass of muscle, fur, and fat were the pups, their squeals occasionally piercing the steaming murmur.

What the sounds didn't say was that we were slowly starving. Each season there were fewer pups because there weren't enough fish for the parents. Fewer of them make it to weaning, and even fewer to yearlings. Every one of us knew it was because of the fish and no one had the courage to say or do anything. And in just a few months, I'd be expected to bring more pups into our home.

Exhausted, I pulled myself onto a spit of sand at the quiet end of the colony, away from everyone else. It would be cold, but at least I'd be able to lick my wounds and maybe even sleep in peace. I spun in a circle to carve myself a nest in the pebbly sand and curled up tight. If any seal had ever earned some rest, it was me.

"We heard everything! Tell us about it!"

Slink, Grace, and Drip wagged their heads at me from a few feet away. I was so tired I didn't even notice them following me.

"If you heard everything, why do I need to tell you about anything?" I snarled, not even trying to be polite. The only things I had in common with these three was that we were all older yearlings and expected to start adding to the colony in a few months. "It's not nice to eavesdrop," I said, sitting up.

"Oh, we didn't eavesdrop," Slink grinned. She'd earned her name because she was skinny and twisted like an eel when she swam. "The whole colony heard. You know how the Old Bull's voice carries at night."

Grace gave me one of her smug smiles, like she should be praised for having the patience to deal with seals like me. "I'm glad you're not hurt...Stump."

"Really, must you call me that?" I said, yanking my half-flipper away from Drip's constantly running nose.

"That's what the Old Bull named you," Grace said. "Those are the rules."

Head low, Drip crept slowly toward my half-flipper again.

"Get away before I tell my friend Balena how good you'd taste."

Drip yelped and hid behind Grace.

"Must you always be so...*abrupt?*" Grace said, nuzzling Drip to settle her down. Grace was always the most dignified and appropriate of all of us. She had this regal air that all but guaranteed she'd end up with one of the ruling bulls. I never liked Grace, but I could never bring myself to hate her. Grace was how things were *supposed* to work and, if I'm honest, how things *did* work when times were good, when fish were plentiful, when the men didn't make it so that all of us—seal, whale, and bear—had to fight harder to survive. But if Grace was part of our system, she was also part of our decline. In seals like her, the system became personal. None of us wanted to swim away from the herd and listen to the Sea and accept that things had changed. Seals like Grace forged ahead, defiant in their belief that everything was fine, or would be, if we just kept our heads down and stayed the course. Maybe I could change that.

"Grace," I said. My flipper throbbed, and I tried my best to rise to her height and look proper. "You're smart." OK, a little lie for the greater good. "You must understand that we're in trouble. That we need to do something."

Grace glanced at Slink and Drip, nervous and flattered that I'd singled her out. "I don't know what you're talking about, Stump."

"The fish, Grace. There are fewer and fewer every new moon."

"The old cows tell us there have been hard times before. We'll be fine," Grace said smoothly, more for Slink and Drip's benefit than mine. Oh, you will make such a handsome queen, Grace.

"It won't be fine unless we *do* something," I said. "We need to *act.*"

Slink and Drip chuffed nervously and shook their necks. Grace nuzzled them. "You know, Stump, you are not without your talents," she cooed, her eyes darting to my flipper. "You could have a good place in the colony if you understood your role in the order of things."

"I'm not like you," I snapped, my patience gone. "I'm not some ambitious, bull-crazy flirt willing to pump out pups who'll end up starving on the beach!"

Slink gasped and Drip crouched further behind Grace.

Grace blinked at me and spoke slowly. "Stump, look at them," she said, tossing her head in the direction of the colony. "They need to believe that there will be a tomorrow, and a next day, and then another. Order comes from confidence, and confidence from stability. All this talk of men, orcas, bears, and starvation undermines that stability, which upsets the order. This will not do. It's why the Old Bull won't listen to you. It's why you lost your flipper."

Slink inched forward, head low. "Don't worry, Stump. We can cover that up. The old cows can do wonders with seaweed and shells. I know that Whiskers and Balls kind of like you. I don't think they'll mind how you look now. And that Whiskers, he'd be quite a catch."

I stared at the three of them, the worst things I could think to say flashing through my head like a school of herring. I sat there until I realized I was crying and had nothing meaningful to say to them anymore. Cold water lapped at my wound and I turned to let the surf pull me away. I headed for a small rock just off the beach, where the cows send their pups when they're acting up. I could be alone there.

* * *

The stars twinkled, and a pink glow had just begun to spread over the colony when I awoke. I rested my chin on the rock and tried not to think about my flipper and the things the Old

Bull and Grace had said. I closed my eyes and tried to remember the Dream Song. Images of Balena and her harem danced and swirled.

"Do you think she's dead?" I heard from the water below. That was Whiskers.

"I don't know. Go and check," said another. That was Balls.

"No, you look."

"You do it!"

"For the love of the Sea, would you both shut up?" I groaned.

Two heads bobbed in the dark waves. "May we?" Balls said.

"You may," I said.

Whiskers and Balls hauled themselves onto the rock next to me. It was high tide and there was just enough room for the three of us. I had to admit it felt good to have two warm bodies against mine. I gazed across the water at the teeming mass on the beach, all that seal-heat. So many pups.

"We heard what the Old Bull told you," Balls said.

We called him that because when we were pups, he found a ball on the beach, some man-toy that had washed up. He and that ball were inseparable. He swam with it, played with it, even slept with it until the Old Bull decided it was silly and tore it to pieces. The ball is gone, but the name stuck. All those months with it had made him the most dexterous seal in the colony. What he lacked in pure intellect, he more than made up for in agility.

"I guess I'm Stump now," I said, lifting my tail.

"I like it," Whiskers said. "It's not one of those regular cow names like Sea Foam or Shell."

"Or Grace," I snapped.

Whiskers rolled his eyes. "No, definitely not like Grace!"

He was Whiskers because his were the longest in the colony. Eyelashes too. It was all the yearlings and cows could talk about. Even though his whiskers never did much for me, I had to admit that he was a good seal, and a *big* one. Big and loyal were the two best words for him. Everyone knew he would be there for you until the end.

Someday Whiskers and Balls would be full-fledged bulls, maybe even the kind who would compete for the colony. That morning on the rock, though, we were still just young enough to call one another friends.

We huddled together as the stars faded and the sun rose behind a smattering of high clouds. I'd just started to doze when Whiskers rose and bent to inspect my flipper.

"Did Balena really do this?" he asked.

I lifted my half-fin to his face and nodded. "She saved my life."

"Why?" Balls asked. "Not that you're not worth saving, Stump." He shot me an apologetic look. "It's just, you know, not something they usually do."

I sat up and looked out over the colony. "She knows something needs to change. She needed me to help her. And I'm going to."

"How?" asked Whiskers.

"I'm going to talk to every able-bodied seal out there," I said, nodding at the crowded beach. "I have six nights until Balena expects me to come with help." Whiskers and Balls exchanged a worried look. "May as well start now," I said.

"Stop. Wait," Whiskers said. He put his large flipper on my back.

"You can't, Stump," said Balls.

"Why the hell not?" I growled.

"The Old Bull," Whiskers said. "He'll kill you, or exile you, if you're lucky. And you won't be," he added, looking at my flipper. "Lucky, that is."

"And Grace has already started talking about how you're 'consorting with killer whales' and 'bargaining with bears.'" Balls shook his head and spat on the rock.

"They're all idiots," I said.

"They're all *scared*," Whiskers said with a long, steamy sigh. "They know everything is wrong, and then you go missing and come home injured and ranting about Balena and the Dream Song and bears and attacking the village."

I tossed myself into the surf. "Is that what I do now?" I shouted. "Rant? Am I like one of those senile old cows the Old Bull leads away from the colony and gives to the Sea?"

All of us were silent, Whiskers and Balls shuffling uncomfortably on the rock while I bobbed in the water.

"I have six nights until the full moon. If I can't get anyone to join me, I'll go myself," I said quietly.

Whiskers shook his head. "Stump, I'm no genius—"

"No argument from me," Balls said.

"—but it's obvious the Old Bull will never do anything to risk his throne," Whiskers said slowly, glancing at Bull Rock in the distance. "Balls and I are already associated with you, and, no offense, that's not good for us."

"Nope, not one bit," Balls shook his head vigorously. "You're political poison, Stump."

Whiskers glared at Balls and then lowered his snout toward me. "Yeah. And you're probably the cleverest seal in the colony. And you're our friend. And," Whiskers rumbled and cleared his throat, embarrassment spreading across his broad face, "we'd never forgive ourselves if you went off into the dark alone."

Balls nudged Whiskers with his snout. "Hey, there, buddy,

uh, this isn't part of the script. We were s'posed to talk her outta—"

"We're going with you, Stump."

"What's that now?" Balls said, bug-eyed.

Whiskers rose to his full height and looked down on Balls. "We're going with her."

ACT III: PART OF THE WHOLE

It wasn't hard to slip away from the colony.

The full moon rose above the coastal mountains, bright enough to cast shadows. The Old Bull and his cronies were bellowing and snorting on their rock as wave after wave of seals returned from the evening hunt. No seal was reported missing and hadn't been for many days.

"The orcas are keeping the truce," I said. Whiskers and Balls shifted nervously.

"Last chance to back out," I said

Balls looked Whiskers up and down and shook his head at me. "Nope. As much as I hate this idea, doing something is better than nothing." He scooped some sand with his flipper and playfully flung it at Whiskers's face. "If king-size here and I are ever going to fight for the colony, there needs to be a colony to fight for. I can't have him coming home a hero while I just rolled in my own piss on the beach!"

"Plus, the three of us will get more done than one, and, no offense, Stump, you're still not moving so great." Whiskers gave me a sympathetic look with his big, weepy eyes.

We took a moment to gaze out on the colony and then let the high tide gently pull us off

the rocky beach.

* * *

{*only three, half-fin?*}

Whiskers and Balls pressed hard against me, trembling.

"You said to bring our best," I answered. "That's us."

Balena responded with a jagged stutter of clicks that seemed to rummage through my head and heart. I wondered whether she could tell from the inside out that I was bluffing, that Whiskers and Balls were all I could scrounge up.

We floated in the surf, a ways out from the beach. Tall black dorsal fins cut the water, circling us. Balena hovered just ahead. She shook her snout, as if to say, *So be it, then.*

I squeezed out from between Whiskers and Balls. "Shall I tell the bears the plan?"

Balena nodded, her toothy mouth opened wide. {*go; be wary; make them understand*}

On the shore were maybe twenty bears. The three large ones I recognized from before, but the rest were the most emaciated, run-down, ragged creatures I'd ever laid eyes on. Sagging skin hung from protruding bones, their once-glowing fur now a mottled blend of white, gray, and a sickly rust. Desperation seemed to drip from their eyes.

Approaching the beach, I began to feel sorry for them until I remembered that a skinny bear is a hungry bear, and a hungry bear is an unpredictable eating machine that probably shouldn't be trusted. But we had no choice.

Whiskers, Balls, and I glided onto the sand, making sure to keep ourselves half in the surf for a quick getaway. The polar bears approached warily, noses high and chuffing in the cold night.

"Is that all?" the lead bear grumbled, scanning the water behind us.

Balls wagged his snout. "Like you all are much to look at!"

I turned and bit down hard on his neck to shut him up. For his part, Whiskers was mostly holding it together, the deep growl caught in his throat barely audible. I had to keep this under control.

"We need to hurry," I barked at the lead bear. "Balena and her guard are waiting."

"What good will the big fish do when we face the men?" the bear sneered.

"She's right over there. You're welcome to swim out and ask her yourself." I scooted aside, as if to welcome him into the surf. Just then, a sleek, lethal shape arced gracefully out of the water and splashed hard onto its back, sending up a great spray that sparkled in the moonlight.

The bear spun round and roared in frustration, "Get on with it then, gimpy!"

I took a deep breath and explained to the bears that they were to move quietly to the edge of the fishing village, nearest the boats.

"Then we attack the town," said a thin, twitchy bear in the back.

"No," I said. "Pay attention."

I explained that from there they would wait for us to take up our positions on the docks. I explained that three seals on the docks would draw little attention if we were seen, but the bears might cause an uproar. They grumbled and postured at that, apparently flattered.

"And then we attack the town," another bear said, "to eat their trash and any slow ones who get in the way."

"No!" I shook my head and spoke slowly. "All of you will block the way to the docks once we start our work, to keep the men away. When the boats are on fire, then you run into the night. Swim if you need to. The orcas will let you pass and might even help you get back here. If we do this right, none of you gets hurt and there will be fish for everyone so you can get nice and fat again."

They looked at one another with sunken yellow eyes and licked their lips, hot, stinking breath curling from their slack mouths. It almost hurt to see how hungry they were.

A couple of grunts from their leader and the bears were trotting toward the twinkling lights of the village. I nodded at Whiskers and Balls before shuffling into the surf. Balena moved in easily beside me.

At first Whiskers wedged himself between us, but she just nudged him away like he was

nothing. I was impressed that he even tried, given how terrified he was of her. Maybe the future-bull had a protective streak.

The massive orca cruised near my half-flipper. I felt proud to no longer be gripped by fear at the sight of Balena, yet there was something unfathomable about her, deep and impenetrable. In the dark water, even my eyes couldn't quite make out her dimensions, her flank a field so perfectly black and vast that I might fall into it if I gazed long enough.

She pulled up next to me, and without knowing why, I dove. Balena shadowed me as we sped downward. Whiskers let loose a panicked bark before everything else faded and soon it was just the two of us speeding through the dark. Balena's side brushed mine, and my fur tingled. This close to her, it was almost as though I didn't have to swim and I could simply let myself be pulled along by her momentum.

"Sing me the Song," I begged, water flowing over my face faster than I'd ever known possible. "The Song, Balena."

A shiver ran down her side, and we slowed until we hung motionless in the murk. Balena turned her head and brought her eye up close. Her mouth parted slowly to reveal her perfect teeth. From somewhere deep within came a sonorous, swirling moan. I wanted to flee, but I was frozen before her, the bone-melting sound more powerful and terrible than a thousand cows wailing over their starved pups, the roars of bears forced to eat their cubs in the hope of another litter next year, the mourning-songs for orcas so skinny they were little more than swimming skeletons. Paralyzed by the Song, I began to sink.

{*i have you, half-fin*} Balena clicked, tucking beneath me to hold me up.

Flopped over her head, I looked straight into her eye. "Why?" I asked. "That wasn't the Whale Song."

{*there are many, many Songs, half-fin, all of them part of the whole*}

"But that one was awful," I said, beginning to feel my body again. "Hideous."

{*yes, all part of the whole, sad and terrible, joyous and carefree; every Song is necessary*}

I let her carry me up, the glow of the starlight slowly growing brighter. I rested my head against her, and that's when I saw it. In Balena's eye bottomless pits of sorrow, innumerable caverns of tragedy, the farthest corners of which were hidden to me. I slid away to face her, just beneath the surface.

"You sang that to prepare me," I said. "To tell me that what we're about to do might be awful, and that you're not sure how it will end."

Balena's mouth opened slightly and she nodded. {*it would be wrong to hide that part of the Song from you, half-fin, you of all the little seals must hear it*}

I thought of the corners of Balena's sorrow that were too dark to make out. "You didn't

sing it all to me."

Balena wagged her jaw, almost certainly a wry smile. {*goodgoodgood, half-fin! now you know that even I cannot see everything; how pointless the Song if we knew where every tide, every current ended?*} She nudged me gently, playfully, with her nose, but I could still see the sadness in her eyes. {*the Sea keeps her secrets, and we deserve to not know all of them*}

We both came up for air and lingered to gaze at the stars. Not far away, Whiskers and Balls bobbed in a grove of swaying dorsal fins. Beyond them, the sparse lights of the village and its docks.

"I think I'm ready, Balena."

At the shallow water our group slowed, and I turned to the whales. Balena glided up close and nudged me with her great snout. She opened her jaws wide, and I was mesmerized by her teeth, white and flawless.

{*good tide and clear water, half-fin—strength*}

I spun and swam hard the rest of the way. The orcas would see that we were not afraid. I wanted Balena to know, most of all.

My courage began to drain when we crawled onto the main wharf, its planks smooth from many years of use. There were four piers extending from the wharf with four docks each. Most of the docks berthed fishing boats, some of which I recognized from our hunts, their nets forcing us farther and farther out. I thought about what it would mean for the colony if these boats no longer stole clouds of fish from the Sea.

Whiskers and Balls huddled close, and we listened and sniffed. The boats pulled lazily at their creaking ropes, the occasional thump of a hull against an old rubber tire or bell clanking. The smell of too-old fish, man sweat, and the sickly sweet tang of oil I remembered from the burning boat.

I turned to Whiskers and Balls. "Do you smell that? It's what we need to start the fires. Come with me."

Shuffling toward the nearest boat, my flipper began to throb, so much so that I had to bite my own tongue to keep from crying out. The sight of shadowy polar bears trotting down the main wharf toward the village helped to distract me from the pain. Even though it was according to plan, doubt nagged at me. Would they do what they'd agreed to? Would they remember that this was about the fish and not revenge?

The gangplank bent under our weight as we boarded the first boat. The deck was littered with rope, netting, and fish the men had carelessly left to die. We scooped as many as we could into our mouths, ravenous. Still chewing, Whiskers and Balls followed me around the boat until we found several lanterns resting on the deck.

"Here, see these? What's inside will burn, even on the water. We need to find as many of these as we can and spill them onto the boats." I tipped over one of the boxes with my snout and stepped back as the amber liquid spread out across the deck.

"Where is the fire?" Whiskers asked, edging backward.

I groaned. That was the part of the plan I hadn't thought of yet: how to start the fire. I had hoped we would find a lit lantern on one of the boats, but now I wasn't so sure.

"Go, both of you! Find as many of these as you can. Spill them on the boats and leave a trail down the ramps to docks and down the docks to the piers. We need a trail that will end here so that the fire will touch everything. Like this," I said, taking up another lantern. Carefully, I tipped it over and shuffled down the ramp, leaving a line of acrid-smelling oil behind me. Whiskers and Balls put the pieces together and followed, each with a lantern in his mouth. Balls balanced a second lantern on his nose as slid down the slick ramp. They passed me quickly on their way to other boats as I traced a thin line of oil toward the main dock.

My flipper screamed in pain, and I paused to rest. From my spot on the wharf, I watched Balls lay a stream of oil down the walkway with one lantern while balancing the other on his head. I couldn't help but laugh. Show-off. Whiskers was already boarding the next boat over in search of more lanterns. My heart swelled. Balls was brash and enthusiastic, whereas Whiskers was more cautious and methodical, but they both went about their work with a sense of purpose. They were here for the colony—but if it weren't for me, they wouldn't be here at all.

A noise to my right caught my attention. In the darkness, the polar bears had set up a ragged picket line between the village and the docks, knowing that the instant they were seen there would be a commotion. They were to weather the storm long enough for us to spread the oil and start the fires.

Rather than sit quietly, the starving bears stalked to and fro, shaking their heads and huffing challenges into the darkness. One bear, a lean adolescent with a rust-colored back, trotted to a large trash bin next to one of the men's structures. With a swipe of his paw, the garbage can went clanging across the narrow street, its contents spilling out across the dirty snow.

Several bears growled and jumped on the trash. Lights came on up and down the street. Nearby a door opened, a man's shape silhouetted against the yellow glow behind him. One of the bears raced toward the door. Before the man could slam it shut, the bear burst in and disappeared into the structure. Screaming pealed through the night, and as if on cue, the bears roared and raced into the village.

"Hurry!" I barked at Whiskers and Balls, no longer worrying about being heard. "The men will come soon!"

Whiskers' head popped up from a boat two berths down. Balls was sniffing at the door of a shed at the far end of the wharf. They both looked at me briefly and then returned to their work, a frantic desperation in their movements.

Ignoring the pain, I shuffled down the wharf to the next pier and boarded the closest boat. Quickly, I found a red container that held enough oil to reach the wharf.

The village was crackling with shouting and running feet. No one had time to worry about the docks. Yet.

At the other end of the wharf, Balls hopped upright from the shed with three red oil containers, one on each flipper and the third on his head. Whiskers took one of the containers from him, bit off the stopper, and began to spill more oil down the nearest dock. When my container was empty, I set it down and froze. There, right in front of me, was a man standing on the dock. He was stretching, facing away from me, arms extended and back arched slightly. It never occurred to me that any of them would sleep on their boats.

As I considered rolling off the dock into the water, the man stiffened up. Shouting and crashing sounds drifted to the boats from the village, and he took two steps toward the wharf. Without thinking, I scooted up from behind and head-butted him into the water between the boats.

The man looked up at me in disbelief, sputtering and cursing in what I could tell were rage-filled words. He paddled clumsily to a dock pile and began pulling himself up when it happened. From beneath a dark, glassy mound of water rose up. A black fin broke the surface, and with barely a ripple, the man was gone. No shout or struggle. Just gone. I'd seen it happen a hundred times, a poor seal—sick, wounded, foolish, or perhaps just young—caught from below by a hungry orca, but never this.

This was not supposed to happen. No one was supposed to get hurt. I vaguely wondered whether this man had pups of his own. Whether they would miss him.

I stumbled to the wharf and dazedly picked up an oil container Whiskers or Balls had left. With it I oiled two more boats and the dock they shared. At the dead-end of the wharf, Balls was rummaging through the shed looking for more containers while Whiskers rushed to finish the last dock.

It occurred to me that at some point I had begun to hear shooting from the village. I bounced between anger and pity at the thought of men using their guns on the bears. How could the men not understand that they had helped to make this happen?

Or was I the one who made this happen?

I forced myself to concentrate on how we would turn the foul-smelling oil into fire. A bear tripped into the open at the village end of the wharf, covered in blood. Two men with guns chased him. He stumbled toward the small sandy beach and collapsed at the edge of the water. The two men raised their guns and watched the bear long enough to confirm he wasn't moving before turning round and running back into the village.

I roared at Whiskers and Balls, "Look for a fire! Any fire! We need to light the oil!"

The three of us bounded up and down the wharf, no longer worried about the noise.

"Nothing!" Balls shouted from the end of the wharf.

"Me neither!" Whiskers answered from somewhere between us.

At the end of a gangway, I heard a voice behind me. A man stood on the deck of his boat pointing at me.

"Какого черта!" he shouted and stepped heavily onto the dock. He held a mean-looking cudgel. A small, white stick dangled from his mouth. The smoke curling from the stick's glowing tip tickled my nose.

"Убирайтесь отсюда!" he yelled again and raised his club, expecting me to flee. Instead, I lunged at his leg and pulled him off balance. His body slammed against the oil-slicked wood. As if in a dream, I watched the small, glowing stick leave his mouth and spin end-over-end through the air to land on the pier.

The oil ignited in a *whoosh*. The man screamed, jumped up, and started to run for his boat, but the line of flame beat him up the ramp. When his pant leg caught fire, he turned and jumped off the dock.

This time I didn't look down into the water.

I watched the orange flames trace a line down the dock to the

pier, turn left, and then sprint toward the wharf, where it turned again and lunged at the shed

Balls had just left. Whiskers rolled out of the way and barked at Balls, who had just enough time

to get free of the shed before it exploded, the sparks and embers rising into the predawn sky. The remaining bears were stumbling back to the small beach. Boat hulls and dock boards and

pilings cracked and groaned.

The growing flames forced me to the edge of the pier. "Time to go!" I barked. The fire crept toward me and I realized, numbly, that my fur was slick with oil. Through the crackling flames and smoke, the reduced, tattered squad of polar bears hit the water, chased by the men with their guns. I looked back to Whiskers and Balls and let out a long, deep call.

"Go!"

* * *

And now I feel them. The bullets.

The first one snaps past my head, but the second, third, and however many more thud into me. For a second, I'm sure they'll pass through like Balena's clicks and whistles, but they slap wetly into me and stay, angry and burning.

I sway. "Go!" It comes out as a croak. The fire reaches me, and the reek of my burning fur fills my head. Maybe I see two seals pushing through flames toward the water when more bullets tear into my side. Maybe not.

Go!

The heat bends the night so that everything twists and quivers. I stumble toward the end of the pier, my flippers sizzling and muscles clenching down on the bullets. With a desperate push, I throw myself into the pure, cool Sea.

I swim as though I have never done anything else. The water behind me glows orange, and the concussions from the explosions punch through me. I swim hard enough to leave the village far behind, far enough to no longer see the unnatural light or feel the blasts.

Whiskers and Balls. They got away. They must have. Please.

I swim through kelp and jellies and then into the open deep where the floes begin to dot the water. But I don't stop to rest, to cool my charred hide or simply let my blood spill out onto the ice. That would be the wrong way to do it. I know I must keep pushing.

I swim for you, so that you will see how strong I am.

I swim until my mouth sputters above the water line, my half-flipper dead and the others moving only through sheer will and pride.

I swim until even the burning in my muscles has left me, the only sensation the water rushing over my face.

I swim until I take one last bite of air in the weak morning light and then slowly sink. I have done my part. You will come now. You must.

Before I can begin pleading, I hear it, the Song. This time it soars to bring down the stars and spread them across the Deep before my fading eyes.

In the quiet darkness, glittering images flash. The Sea is a spinning galaxy of fish. The Old Bull is gone. In his place sit two silhouettes on Bull Rock, one hulking and steady, the other sleek and graceful. They are scarred, well-fed, and wise. They remember me with fondness and respect. The colony is whole and prosperous. And who can sleep for all the pups!

{*half-fin...*}

From the depths something massive rushes upward, so fierce the water flees before it. Its Song both swaddles and pierces me.

All I wanted was to change things, Balena. To make a difference. To be a part of something before the end.

{*every Song is part of the whole; you and I shall sing your ending, half-fin; sing with me*}

My open mouth makes no sound in the blackness, but I know she can hear the music in my heart. I sink like a stone. She is coming. I am ready.

Breaking through the cloudy murk, her teeth, her perfect teeth.

10
STUD

Insecure, horny, and bored. Three states of mind that lead fourteen year-olds to bad decisions.

"You can do this," I whispered, rocking on the edge of my bed.

The ice cube rested on my thigh, a dark water stain spreading across my jeans as it melted. Between my index finger and thumb, I tugged on my half-frozen earlobe. In the other hand, my mother's sewing needle. I raised it to eye-level. The needle's tip glinted in the light from the bare bulb above my head.

"Do it, do it, do it." I closed my eyes, held my breath, and pushed.

Give me a fight in the cafeteria with Roberto, Manuel, or DeAndre. Any. Fucking. Day. This was worse than getting my nose broken and reset.

When the needle was about halfway through, I collapsed onto my bed. I think I let out a whimper.

"'Ey! What's going on in there?" my mother called out from the hallway.

"Yuck, Mom," Cami said. "Let him have his privacy. At least the hormonal little pig thought to close the door."

A warm rivulet crept down my neck. "Pretty sure I'm bleeding now!" I yelled.

"¡Guácala, sinvergüenza!" Several heavy steps and a bang from farther down the hall. No one slammed a door like my mother.

I cursed and gave it one last push. The needle exited my earlobe with a moist pop and jabbed into my neck. "Ay, *shit!*" I screamed.

"Pervert!" Cami hollered out in the hallway.

* * *

A half-hour later I stumbled out of my bedroom, pale, sweaty, and triumphant. After the needle, fitting the ruby stud I had bought at Eastridge Mall was a piece of cake. Every inch of skin, from the top of my head to my shoulder, was a war zone of pain, but it would be worth it, I told myself. I smiled as I sauntered into the kitchen for more ice.

I'm gonna look so *chingón* at school on Monday if I can get this swelling down, I thought.

At the kitchen table, Cami sat holding a bottle of Pepsi to the side of her face. The corner of her mouth slanted into a knowing grin. "I hope you had your fun."

I leaned into the freezer and turned my head to face her, the cold mist soothing my ruined ear. "You seriously think that's how I sound when I'm wrestling the priest?" I said, grabbing an ice tray.

"Wrestling the pr—? *Shit*, Dani, you are going straight to hell."

I dropped the ice tray hard onto the counter and pried out a cube. The left side of my head exploded with new pain when it touched my ear. Only the satisfaction of grossing out Cami kept me from fainting.

Cami's mouth fell open at the sight of the ruby stud. "I hope you know what you've gotten yourself into, dumbass," she said and took a sip from her bottle.

"Don't blame me for looking so good." My earlobe howled, but no way I was going to let it show in front of her.

She shook her head and stood up from the table. "You're so cool now we're gonna have to call you *culón*. Look, I'm going over to Leticia's so I don't have to see your ginger-ass dad when he comes to get you today, but good luck explaining *that* thing in your ear."

The ice cube slipped from my fingers and skittered across the floor. Cami's huge brown eyes mocked me from across the kitchen.

"Bill's coming," I whispered.

"Yup," she nodded. "Today. And you know how he feels about *maricas*."

Queers?

Cami reached up and gently fingered the ruby stud. "For what it's worth," she said, "I think it looks hella sexy."

* * *

All afternoon my mother stalked the house, her hooded eyes scanning every room for some invisible threat. Days like those I made damn sure to stay out of her way.

"*¿Dónde chingaos está?*" she said, checking the street from the front window. "He was supposed to be here hours ago."

I had eavesdropped on the phone negotiations that led up to today. Final terms were agreed upon earlier in the week. Bill would pick me up Saturday, at ten. I would stay the

TOMAS BAIZA

night with him in Santa Cruz and be home by five p.m. Sunday, in time for dinner.

The non-negotiables, Mom said, you good-for-nothing son-of-a-bitch: There will be no alcohol, no visits with buddies, no leaving your fourteen year-old son in the van while you're in some bar, no dropping him off with acquaintances or dumping him alone at the apartment while you 'take care of errands.'

To sum up, there would be absolutely no reason for concern about Bill's conduct or my safety, or my mother would use every resource at her disposal to make things right. And did he remember that she's a social worker who could bring down on him the full weight of the system to protect her son and make his life a living hell?

It was past noon now. I sat sweating in the kitchen, trying to not mess with my ear. It throbbed like someone had taped an M-80 to the side of my head and set it off.

"The *hell* were you thinking when you decided to do that?" my mother said. "You really want to look like one of those thug *pandilleros* your sister has chasing after her?" She shook her head at me from the living room. "Serve you right if your ear fell off, *pendejo.*"

My mother stepped back from the window, chin high. "Ahí 'stá." She looked at me and thrust a hand into her purse. "It's been almost two years since we've done this, but you remember how it goes: I'm giving you money. Twenty this time. You come home with twenty dollars. If you don't come home with twenty dollars, it's because you had to spend it to come home."

My mother pushed the bill into my hand and padded down the hall, stopping in the doorway to her bedroom. She looked at me with red eyes. She looked ten years older than she did only a minute ago. "Just come home," she said before closing her door.

The doorbell rang. I grabbed my Converse duffle bag and opened the front door just as Bill was flicking a cigarette butt into the pot of geraniums that my mother kept on the front step. A shot of adrenaline ran through me, like usual when I hadn't seen him in a while. Gray streaks had begun to colonize his red beard, and the wrinkles around his eyes were a little more defined. Levi's hugged his skinny thighs. He liked his jeans dark, but they were always faded beneath the knees where the lineman spikes he wore to climb telephone poles had rubbed the denim thin. His tan Pac Bell work shirt was unbuttoned to the middle of his broad, flat chest. The embroidered name tag that read *BILL* in red cursive had begun to come up in the corner.

It felt strange to think that he had a job where people knew him as work-Bill. What was work-Bill like? Was he anything like bar-Bill, hungover-Bill, or dangerous-Bill?

As always, though, my eyes were drawn most to his hands and forearms. No matter how much Bill ate, drank, or smoked, he was always lean. Shirts hung on him like from a hanger, and his narrow waist was almost delicate, but from his elbows to his fingertips, everything looked forged from steel. Knotted forearms with veins thick enough to cast shadows against his sunburned skin swung at his side and ended in broad palms that sprouted trunks for fingers.

My memories of our visits were dictated by what those hands did while we were together, whether they patted me on the head or bound my arms behind my back and forced me to fight my way loose. Sometimes they would give me a dollar for a milkshake, other times they would cuff me across the cheek for dropping my guard. Whether they dealt out kindness or violence, they always gave off the stale essence of unfiltered Camels.

"Hey," Bill said.

"Hey." My face went hot and my ear burned.

"Where's your mother?"

"Asleep," I lied.

Bill looked me up and down. "You ready?"

I up-nodded him, like I would some random guy on the street. It felt weird and his expression told me he sensed it, too. I grabbed my Converse duffle and shut the door behind me. There were no words exchanged when I passed him on the way to the van, but I could feel him watching me.

"You've gotten big," he said from behind.

Bill's van, a white Ford Econoline, was parked in front of the house. I climbed in, tossed the bag in the footwell, and looked around the cab. It hadn't changed since the last time I sat in it. The competing odors of cigarettes and canned shoe-string potatoes filled the cab. I inspected the engine shroud between the seats that doubled as his mobile desk where he kept his notebooks and pens, extra packs of Camels, an old glass ashtray announcing 'Stolen from SAMBO'S Bakersfield, Calif.' on the bottom, and a hand-copied poem by some guy named Robert Burns.

We cam na here to view your warks,
In hopes to be mair wise,
But only, lest we gang to hell,
it may be nae surprise.

Every time I sat in that van, I would pick up the powder blue notebook paper to read that poem and try to connect it to Bill, to this man who biology defined as my father. What was it about those verses that resonated with him? Did they have anything to do with me? Every time I returned the poem to its place behind the ashtray, I would have more questions than answers.

Bill climbed into the driver's seat and lit a cigarette. If it's anything like the last couple of visits, I would read the Burns poem for a few minutes and probably he wouldn't try to small talk until we got to 680 South.

"Hey," he said.

I looked up from the poem.

"What's that?" Bill reached across the cab and flicked my left ear. His middle finger was hard and cigarette-stained and felt like a club across the side of the face.

"Nothing," I grunted.

"Looks like an earring."

I nodded and focused again on the poem written on wrinkled notebook paper and stained with dried coffee rings.

Bill blew smoke out his nose. The air in the cab grew thick and I told myself that I was big enough now. Maybe I couldn't take him yet, but I was certain I could at least make it out of the van in one piece.

"What does that *mean*?" he said slowly.

"What does *what* mean?"

"That," he said and jabbed his finger at my ear. "You wouldn't have it if you weren't trying to say something by it. That's not a Mexican thing, is it?"

I forced myself to look him in the eye. They were my eyes, only icy blue. "It's just a ruby stud," I say.

He held his cigarette out the window and stared forward. "The only guys I know who have earrings are hippies or faggots —and you don't look like a hippy."

I looked over at Bill, seated behind the wheel. Why do we even do this? I wondered. Why did my mother put herself through hell to arrange these visits? Why did Bill bother to show up? What did any of us get out of these performances other than being able to look in the mirror and claim that we did what we were supposed to do?

"You saying I look like a faggot?"

"Maybe," Bill said.

Sitting in that cluttered, sour-smelling Econoline van, it slowly dawned to me that there was nothing forcing us to do any of it. I knew, right then and there, that this shit was entirely optional. I could make it end today.

I took a deep breath. "And what if I was?"

Bill's blue eyes caught fire. He took a long drag from his cigarette and looked me over from head to toe. "Are you?"

I turned in my seat to face him. "What would you do if I said 'yes'?" I waited for him to answer, but he just blinked at me while the ash on his cigarette burned longer. "What if I told you that I had a boyfriend? That I shave my balls for him and that we do it every day before my mom gets home from work?" Bill's eyes got wider and my ears rang from fear. Any second, I thought, the rock-hard back of his hand would connect with my temple. "What would be worse," I said, "if I told you that I like it on the bottom, or that when I give him a blowjob I always makes sure he goes all over my face?"

Bill flipped his cigarette out the window and stared straight ahead. His forearms flexed as he gripped the steering wheel. I pretended to read the Burns poem.

"I think maybe you should go back inside," he said.

I stared at my lap and waited for him to change his mind, to tell me that none of it mattered and that we should go to Santa Cruz anyways. For a second, I think I actually convinced myself that's what I wanted.

"Okay," I said.

Hands trembling, I slipped my fingers to the top of the page and pulled. The Burns poem tore neatly in two. I squared the halves and pulled them apart again, and again, until I had turned the page into confetti. With a flick of my wrist, I tossed the power blue shreds into the air and watched them settle onto the engine shroud, amongst the random possessions Bill had accumulated over the years that gave him a sense of order and meaning.

The things that meant most to him.

* * *

From the curb, I watched as my father's white Econoline drove away. Just before it disappeared around the corner, Bill's scent overwhelmed me, as if he had never left. There on the pavement was his cigarette, a thin wisp of smoke curling up from the end of the butt. I stepped into the street and stood over it. With the toe of my shoe, I slowly ground the butt into the blacktop until nothing was left.

My mother was still in her room when I went back inside. I sat at the kitchen table holding an ice cube to my ear. The tears came, but it was okay because no one was there to see. The price you pay for cool, I thought.

In my pocket, I felt the money. If I cried hard enough, maybe, just maybe, my mother would let me keep the twenty dollars.

11

AND THEN A WIND

Just before the train emerges from the tunnel comes a breeze that swells into a gust and then a wind. Some mornings it's hot, others cool. Either way, it helps me figure out what kind of day it's going to be.

I can feel its first whisper on my face now, flowing from the tunnel and down the channel that soon will be stuffed by a speeding train occupying every square inch between the platform and the far wall. Last week a woman's terrier broke loose and chased a rat down there. A couple of us jumped onto the tracks and got the dog out just before the train burst out of the dark. It was exhilarating and terrifying, that stirring of air.

Like there was something inevitable in it.

But I can't decide whether this morning's breeze is hot or cold because I'm a little distracted just now. There you are, walking towards me. Your dazzling, up-and-coming sales manager smile outshines the train's lights winking in the tunnel behind you. You wave your gloved hand. Like we're friends. Like we have a connection because you work with my wife.

Ah, Kenneth. I think you have no idea. It seems you're

unaware that she and I have had, you know, The Talk. About the conference, the hotel bar, the knock on her door later that night, the separate Ubers back to the airport. There've been tears. A few rough weeks. Our kids are quiet at the dinner table now.

And in the bedroom it's...well, let's just say it's like you're there and I'm not into threesomes.

The breeze picks up and makes the sweat on my forehead tingle. You call out my name and I marvel at the pure, uncomplicated warmth of your voice as it competes with the surge of possibilities from the tunnel.

I read this morning that police narrowly averted an act of violence in the London Tube. Don't you love that they call it The Tube, Kenneth? That literal Brit whimsy. We just call ours BART.

How utterly boring. We really do need to spice things up somehow.

The gust is now a true rush, the force of it ruffling your long coat and curly blonde hair. Could you be any more handsome? I can see what my wife saw in you. What she still sees when you pass in the hallways or glance at one another in meetings.

Those broad shoulders block sight of the train as it leaps from the tunnel. You've shifted your briefcase from one hand to the other and you're coming in for the shake, elbow bent, shoulder cocked at that angle. Just so. The way men do.

The wind has become a hurricane. I take your hand firmly in mine, glance down at the tracks. I think of the terrier and the rat.

And the inevitable wind.

Ah, Kenneth, damn our luck. This wind is hot. It is so unbearably hot.

12
A RECKONING

The screaming began on a Monday.

Ghislaine had just started down the hill with the twins when her world turned sideways. Pulling away from the house, it was barely a ringing in her ears, the kind that might come and go without notice. Halfway down the hill, however, it intensified, the ringing swelling into a howl. Ghislaine squinted through the pain, her eyes watering so badly the road ahead narrowed into a gauzy, curving ribbon of agony. Twice she felt the SUV's tires rub the curb.

"Mommy!" one of the girls chirped as a new, even more frightening level of torture began to unravel in Ghislaine's head.

Regret. Guilt. Paralyzing disappointment.

"Mommy!"

Fear focused Ghislaine long enough to pull to the side of the road. The SUV lurched to a stop. Ghislaine buried her face in her hands and rubbed her temples hard enough to hope that she could push out the fading pain. She managed a glance in the rearview. The twins appeared unaffected by the tumult and could only watch in confusion from the back seat.

"Are you two alri—" Ghislaine started to ask when something skidded past her window, missing them by inches. Ghislaine watched the fishtailing car spin and come to rest against a parked truck. Not a collision so much as a hard meeting of sheet metal and plastic.

The driver—a neighbor Ghislaine recognized but had never properly met—stumbled from the vehicle and fell onto the curb, holding her head. Ghislaine considered checking on the woman when she heard the sirens coming up the hill. An ambulance raced past followed by two police cruisers, one of them stopping in front of the woman's car. Just as quickly as the emergency vehicles arrived, the wailing from up the hill began to fade and her head started to clear. She sat in the new silence working her jaw and rubbing her forehead.

The girls eyed her nervously in the rearview.

Pull it together, *m'ija*, her father would have said.

She forced a smile into the mirror. "Todo está bien, niñas. Don't worry, 'kay? Everything's alright."

Ghislaine slipped the SUV into neutral and let it coast past the police car to join the line of others streaming down the hill.

Is everything alright? Ghislaine asked herself.

* * *

The origins of the screaming would at first be erroneously attributed to the underpaid driver of a Caterpillar backhoe who was ordered to knock down a stand of trees. The wall of Western white pines guarded the hillside that would become the neighborhood's next phase advertised by a hastily erected sign:

COMING IN 2021: WHITEHILL HEIGHTS, PHASE II
RESERVE YOUR LOT TODAY AND ENJOY
THE VIEW FROM THE TOP!

Even before the tractor's front bucket dug into the first pine's soft bark, a blanket of unease spread over the workmen. Beneath the din of saws and heavy machinery, a low whine crept from the woods, growing into a howl and then an oscillating scream. Nausea churned in the workers' bowels, their eyes squeezed shut and minds scrambled by the dismaying melange of wild anger and regret. The tree tipped to forty-five degrees before the tractor jerked to a halt in a cloud of dust and diesel exhaust. The driver fell from the cab and rolled in the dirt as a wet stain spread across the back of his jeans.

From the shelter of their vine-shaded pergolas, Whitehill residents watched as the convoy of battered pickups and economy cars sped downhill from the worksite, tires squealing in blatant disregard for Association rules. They scowled at one another from their manicured yards, unsure whether to be relieved or frightened by the sudden exodus of laborers.

What do you think that's all about? one man asked. We really should inform the contractor. Or ICE, said another, hands on hips. None of them can be here legally.

The residents of Whitehill pursed their lips and bobbed their heads in agreement when one of them froze. What's that? he asked. The others stared blankly into the air, their growing uneasiness triggering a sudden flight response. Snippets of past iniquities, wrongdoings, hurts and regrets, flashed through their minds as their temples began to pound and bowels turned to jelly.

Excuses were made, eye contact avoided, doors slammed. Soon, Whitehill cowered beneath an orange sun made sinister by the wailing from the woods that grew slightly more urgent and went on longer every day.

* * *

"How you been holdin' up, sugar, what with all the fuss lately?"

Ghislaine smiled at Blanche, grateful for the distraction. Though it was barely a ten-minute walk to Alex's house, Ghislaine found her mother-in-law's periodic silence even more disconcerting than her occasionally off-kilter take on things. Plus, she was starting to find some comfort in Blanche's syrupy Southern drawl. With Carl gone so often, Blanche was the only other adult in the house to talk to.

"I'm okay. As long as I get the kids away in time, it's just a matter of waiting it out." They walked some more, taking in the evening air. "You know...you could come with us," Ghislaine said suddenly. "Why do you insist on staying home when it happens?"

Blanche shook her head. "Dunno. It don't seem right to run away—not that I judge you," she added with a sincere glance at Ghislaine. "When it gets too much, I just throw on those fancy headphones the girls use to watch—what the hell is it again?"

"YouTube."

"That's it, YourTube. D'ya know they play songs, too? I just find some songs and gut it out when it gets to be too much."

"Well, I hope you know you don't have to stay at home. I hate the thought of you suffering through it."

"Child," Blanche said with a casual wave of her hand, "if I ran away from every single thing that caused a fuss, I wouldn't be able to call this a life, now would I?"

* * *

"Your mother-in-law seems disoriented," Alex said, looking through the French doors. Outside, Blanche walked the perimeter of Alex's kidney-shaped pool, slightly bent, but with a vigor that belied her age. "No offense, Ghislaine, but she can have a chilling effect on the ambience."

Ghislaine took a small sip of wine. "Leave her alone. She's only been with us for a few months and she's still culture-shocking. This place is nothing like where she came from."

"Is *anywhere* like Kentucky?" said Alex, swirling his cognac. "Couldn't you have left her home with the kids?"

Ghislaine felt her scalp prickle. There was something unnerving about Alex bringing up her children. "Carl's away and my daughters are at a sleepover," she said, staring at Blanche. "I didn't want to leave her alone."

"How is ol' Carl?" asked Alex, pretending to watch Blanche but side-eying the slightly-built, attractive woman next to him.

Ghislaine finished her wine and handed the glass to him. "I'm going to check on her."

The nightbirds had begun to sing and a breeze snaked through the honey locusts that towered over the backyard.

Ghislaine watched Blanche pace slowly around the pool, occasionally fixating on the small, pointed leaves dotting the water like confetti. The old woman may as well have been a Martian she was so strange to Ghislaine. Still, there was something familiar about her *suegra*'s alienness, something that resonated in a way that both unnerved and intrigued her.

"Can I get you anything, Blanche? Something to drink?"

Blanche stopped. "This is where it happened," she said carefully, eyes on the water.

"Where what happened?" Ghislaine knew precisely what Blanche was asking about.

"Where Mr. Alex's wife passed."

"Yes, from what I've heard," Ghislaine nodded quickly. "She was a nice woman, the few times she and I met. I've heard more about it from others than him. He doesn't talk about it."

Blanche nodded and resumed her purposeful, clockwise stroll around the pool.

Ghislaine fidgeted. "Do you want anything?"

Blanche closed her eyes and lifted her face to the evening breeze. "How 'bout some of that *good* whiskey Mr. Alex keeps behind that fancy bar of his" she said dreamily. "The hell that foreign stuff called? The Suntory."

"Uh, okay," Ghislaine answered, a shiver running through her. How in the world could Blanche know about that? "I'll be right back," she said hesitantly and turned towards the house.

It occurred to Ghislaine that the fact she herself knew about the Suntory was just as troubling.

* * *

Although it was summer, Alex had turned on the fireplace and opened the French doors to let the gas flames compete with the cool evening air. Ghislaine stood next to the fire, cradling her tumbler.

She scanned the room, her expression an exquisite resting bitch face. Neighbors—some she knew, most she didn't, really—engaged in all manner of vapid exchanges, intellectual jousts, passive rivalries, flirtations, both overt and covert. After a year, Ghislaine had begun to not care whether she would ever fit in with these people. Sure, she was different from them, she thought, but at some point familiarity, if not actual intimacy, should help bridge the gaps, right?

Her mother-in-law's arrival shattered that delusion.

Ghislaine made her way back to the open patio doors. Blanche had given up circling the pool and sat on a bench, beside her an empty shot glass. The image made Ghislaine's breath catch in her throat: an old woman, out of her element, sitting alone.

Will that be me someday? she wondered.

In her neighbors' reaction to Blanche, Ghislaine recognized the othering to which she had been subjected and, as much as she fought to deny it, still felt. The side-long glances, the clumsy avoidance of certain topics and fixation on others, the occasional enthusiastic *¡Hola!* or *¡Buenos días!* There was hardly a conversation that didn't involve some subtle form of appropriation or erasure.

A deep voice interrupted her spiraling thoughts.

"What do Appalachia and dementia have in common?" Alex asked.

Ghislaine let the last of the bourbon slide past her tongue and rounded on her neighbors. "What, Alex?" she asked sharply. Her lips felt numb. "What, precisely, do they have in common?"

Alex aimed a grin at her. "Both represent a fundamental break from reality, a retreat from the world of the rational to the existentially surreal."

Guests smiled, eager to ingratiate themselves with their host and one another. Alex polished off his brandy with a wink at Ghislaine. She scowled into her glass and wished, for the umpteenth time, that Carl were there to defend his own mother.

* * *

Ghislaine snuck a careful glance at Alex—handsome, fifteen years her senior, and widowed a year ago. His wife, Kara, had been unpretentious and heartbreakingly kind. Ghislaine felt an immediate rapport with this down-to-earth, attentive woman and latched onto her in the weeks after she and Carl had moved to Whitehill. Ghislaine wept when she heard the news of Kara's drowning and regretted that they'd only met a few times for coffee.

"I hope you're liking it here," Kara had said at their last meeting.

"It's—it's been good," Ghislaine responded, fumbling with her cup. "We're settling in." She could feel Kara's eyes on her.

"Well, when we first arrived in Whitehill—what, ten years ago?—I was adrift. All the teas, tent parties, soirées. Everyone in one anothers' business. It was all a bit much."

Ghislaine laughed nervously. "I thought it was just me."

Kara reached across the table to cover Ghislaine's hand with hers. "Dear, no! This is a strange place where—" Kara's lips stretched tight. "Where people just don't seem to...*reflect*, to think about what things mean. It's like everyone's personal attic is stuffed to the rafters with discarded junk that just sits there. It's very hard to explain."

"My father once told me that if you don't take the time to look around you, life could pass you by."

"Sounds like a wise man—with good taste in 80s movies," Kara giggled.

For the first time since she and Carl had arrived, Ghislaine dared to hope she might be making a friend.

* * *

At first, Ghislaine had found it surprisingly easy to overlook Alex's occasional callousness. He had mourned, she thought, with a dignity that hid his loneliness.

Lately, though, she'd begun to wonder whether he really was lonely.

"You are so full of it, sometimes," Ghislaine smirked.

"And yet you find me irresistible," Alex winked.

Ghislaine watched the other guests pretend not to notice. "Makes me think of the screaming," she said suddenly, as if she were pulling the pin on a grenade. "Normality seems to fly out the window when that starts up."

Alex winced at the faux pas. Everyone knew not to broach that topic at the neighborhood gatherings. So much easier to mock an easy target like Ghislaine's mother-in-law than deal with the elephant in every room.

"Yes, well," Alex said, accepting a refresh of brandy, "let's not dwell too much on that. I still contend it was those workmen who started it. Once those people are gone, every-thing should return to normal. You speak Spanish, don't you? You could walk up there and find out what their plans are."

Asshole, Ghislaine fumed. The fact that she had given Alex a blowjob earlier that day, hurriedly before the screaming began, made her stomach turn. It wasn't the fact of it that disgusted her so much as having done it—for a few months now —with *him*. At first, she found him attractive in that safe way one looks at a silly crush. Then, after Kara, she had convinced herself it was compassion and bonding over the isolation. Behind all of it, a festering resentment of Carl and the passive, alienating judgement of her neighbors.

Ghislaine tumbled into memories of her father.

Ghilly, baby, you're special, he had told her once. It'll be hard, but you'll find your way to do great things.

Here in Alex's spacious home, uttering inanities with familiar strangers, her husband a thousand miles away, the twins at a sleepover, her strange mother-in-law out back communing with whatever it was that flowed through her, Ghislaine seethed.

I'm sorry, Daddy.

Perfect acrylic nails dug into her palm until it felt as if they might break skin. It was one thing screwing Alex when life was normal, drab, a solid, unchanging baseline in need of augmentation. It was another when, for six hours a day now, the world was thrown into turmoil. A frivolous, soul-deadening dalliance in an existence now threatened to its core by the screaming.

Ghislaine prepared a blistering riposte to Alex, the kind her father would have called one of her 'world-ending *chingazos*.'

In the time it took to run her tongue over her lips, she noticed all eyes on her, everyone waiting to see what the exotic woman would do, a silent consensus among them that she was now responsible for what everyone was about to feel. How many times had she been put in that position and tucked tail? Are you ready to shit all over these people? Ghislaine wondered. It's not like they wouldn't deserve it...

Fighting to control her breathing, Ghislaine turned to look out onto the patio again. The bench was vacant but for a small, empty shot glass. "Oh, crap. Where's Blanche got off to now?"

* * *

Blanche stopped to gaze up at the tree-covered hill. Early stars shone above the pines, their faint sparkle a stark contrast to the woods' smothering darkness. Ghislaine would scold her for wandering off again, she knew, but it was getting more and more infuriating to watch the fakery at these get-togethers.

Goose pimples prickled down her arms. It still surprised her how cool the nights were here. Not like back home, she thought. Evenings on the porch, sweating to the symphony of crickets, the fireflies tracing white-green threads through the dense, humid air. Those nights, seated next to Leonard and looking out into the moist blackness, her husband might come close to being the man she'd first met.

Blanche had never thought of herself as an optimist. Still,

she nurtured a persistent hope that somewhere, somehow, two people could come together and it wouldn't eventually go bad. When Leonard went bad, he went all the way, she thought.

She closed her eyes and fought to hold the memories at bay. Flailing fists. Oxygen tanks. Nose tubes. The pillow. Go ahead, he wheezed. Do it.

Blanche pulled her shawl tighter and glared at the woods. "Everybody has their reckonin'," she growled at the wall of trees. Her lips trembled. "Why like this!" Her shout, weakened by decades of cigarettes and alcohol, came out as little more than a hiss. She quailed at the idea that, every day when the screaming pierced the neighborhood, it reserved a special part of itself just for her.

A voice reached Blanche, both unexpected and welcome. The trees? she wondered. No, it came from behind. Ghislaine was calling for her. Poor thing, Blanche thought. Isn't it enough that she cat-herds the kids with no help from Carl without having to chase down her weird mother-in-law?

Blanche spared one last look at the woods. "See you tomorrow, you son of a bitch," she mumbled before shuffling back down the sidewalk.

* * *

"Better hurry if you're gonna get the kids to that fancy camp before the hollerin' sets in today." Blanche stroked the girls' heads as she walked the three of them out to the driveway. The twins waved quickly before clambering into the SUV. Blanche gave them a distracted smile and turned to look uphill, towards the trees.

The old woman's expression—a grim mixture of revulsion and defiance—caught Ghislaine off guard. Since she had come to live with them, Ghislaine quietly pitied her uncultured mother-in-law. In that moment, though, her condescension gave way to familiarity. There was something about the old woman, unfathomable and strange, that both fascinated and frightened her. A memory pushed itself up.

La curandera, she realized. Blanche reminds me a little of Doña Maritza.

"You'll be okay?" Ghislaine asked, struggling to steady her voice.

"I'll be fine," Blanche said. "It ain't hurt nobody yet. Not for real, anyways." She nodded at her grandchildren. "Best they don't have to witness it, though. G'on."

Ghislaine glanced doubtfully towards the woods and then at Blanche. "No, I mean, you'll go back inside, right? No wandering the neighborhood? Carl texted that he might not make it home tonight and we can't have you getting—" her mouth snapped shut at the memory of the police search and finding Blanche half-conscious and only partially clothed on the edge of the woods.

"Stop it," Blanche snarled with a flick of the wrist. "I'll be fine. G'on, get 'em out of here."

* * *

Blanche watched the SUV until it disappeared around a corner. The mid-morning sun warmed her face for several minutes until she heard it, the first traces of a sound that tip-toed the line between mourning and threat. Still in her night-gown and slippers, she padded up the block as the sound swelled and the very air began to throb. Around her, neighbors fled into their houses or threw themselves into cars, radios blasting against closed windows as they raced down the hill to improvised coffee dates or rescheduled yoga classes.

Blanche stopped and glared at the woods. The screaming

seemed to shake the needles of every tree until they became a blur, a quivering semblance of the pines they had been moments before. Through the green mist the sound opened its eye to her.

Her stomach lurched and she clamped down to keep from soiling herself. Frozen in place, Blanche gritted her teeth and resisted until something deep inside gave way. For the first time in ages, she could see—truly *see*—just like when she was younger, the way she used to see that got her in trouble and made her feared. *Momma, Uncle Ricky shouldn't use the chainsaw tomorrow. Momma, Daddy needs to dig a hole because Rosco is gonna get into the rat poison. The president shouldn't oughta go to Dallas, Momma. Momma, why will you get sick?*

If the weight of time and life's burdens had dimmed her ability to see, the screaming had woken it up again. She felt a hot wetness trickle down her leg.

No, goddamnit! a corner of her mind protested, but the rest was overtaken by visions...

...a body floating in a pool, long blonde hair fanned out in sparkling water. A man standing in the shallow end. Cut to two naked bodies writhing. A ceiling fan wobbling above them in a dark room. Blood...

Stumbling in her slippers, Blanche repeated *no-no-no* until she reached the house. She wept in the shower as the screaming rose in intensity. Wrapped in a towel, she dragged herself to the laptop and clutched at the headphones until she was lost in music. She never much cared for Merle Haggard, but somehow "Sing Me Back Home" seemed to fit the occasion.

Blanche's last shredded visions before losing consciousness were of an oxygen mask, bloodshot eyes, and a hovering pillow.

"Do it," the eyes said.

* * *

It was six weeks into the screaming when the cable television crew arrived in their white rental van.

After several days of roaming the neighborhood, aggressively interviewing imperious and guarded Whitehill residents, the four self-styled cryptozoologists parked their van at the abandoned construction site, made a show of inspecting their cameras and infrared lenses, and marched dramatically into the woods.

For the first and only time in the show's run, the broadcast would be live-streamed. Viewers watched the team's morning hike to what they thought might be the epicenter of the phenomenon. In a shallow, bowl-like depression ringed by the forest's largest and oldest pines, the bigfoot hunters chattered excitedly, with the group's leader declaring the site 'particularly squatchy.' The members exchanged observations and theories for several minutes before falling silent, unnerved by some change in their surroundings.

The broadcast ended abruptly some sixty-three seconds into the screaming.

Two of the team were later discovered side-by-side in their soiled underwear, rigid hands forced into one another's faces and guts, as if clawing their way into the other might protect them from the assault. The hulking, slow-witted member who provided the show's comic relief they discovered several hundred yards away, disemboweled by his own hands.

The handsome real scientist and only female team member they never found at all.

* * *

A small, prosperous enclave, hermetically sealed from the outside by asking price, property taxes, privilege, and delusion.

For the past year, Blanche had wandered the leafy neighborhood while her son was lost to meetings or conferences (and whatever else he'd gotten himself into), her granddaughters were at school or playdates (or wherever), and her daughter-in-law was doing errands or exercise classes (or whatever else she'd gotten herself into).

It never seriously occurred to Blanche to tell Carl about his wife's recent extracurriculars. Sorry, boy, she thought. You gotta be present to win.

And she had to live somewhere.

Blanche meandered the curving streets, allowing herself to think of her late husband only occasionally before focusing on mundanities like weeds encroaching on flowerbeds, new cars gathering dust in driveways, once well-kept bird feeders choked with cobwebs, arguments filtering through open kitchen windows or over backyard fences. Blanche had witnessed more of these scenes since the screaming had begun as nerves frayed to the breaking point. The mail carriers, with whom she'd struck up acquaintanceships during her walks, now rushed past, harried expressions showing the strain of having to finish their rounds before mid-morning. Some days the mail didn't come at all.

For all her wandering, Blanche still felt as if she walked the surface of an alien world, the topography increasingly familiar, but somehow off, the atmosphere breathable, but probably toxic over the long term. Blanche didn't want to die here, a stranger in a strange land.

Twice, early on, she'd got caught out when her ears began to ring and the moaning rose above the wind and birds. Too far from the house and decades beyond running, she squeezed her eyes shut and forced herself to move forward, one foot after the other, her bowels churning. The first time Blanche awoke to a police man kneeling over her, the reflection in his mirrored sunglasses reminding her just how old she was. The second time was no picnic, either, but at least she'd made it home. *Like a buzzard on a meat truck,* she remembered her mother saying once about an inescapable suffering. That's what it felt like. The screaming drove into her and pried her open, a psychotic surgeon performing a vivisection on her soul, exposing her to what squirmed inside.

Both times she felt the hard shell she'd erected around her ability to *see* being forced open—and with that sight came the guilt. She thought she was too old, too jaded, too mean, to feel it anymore. But the screaming proved meaner than her. No, not mean, she knew. Uncaring. Utterly dispassionate and unrelenting in the despair it brought. Every wrong thing she had ever done to herself or others was laid bare.

Under full assault from the screaming, Blanche felt a deep sense of awe at her shame for Ghislaine. This young woman she hadn't liked at first—whip smart, eerily pretty, standoffish— had somehow won her over without trying.

Blanche wondered if that was what it meant to love: to hurt as badly for others' sins as for your own.

* * *

"Why are you looking at me like that?"

Sugar meant for coffee spilled onto the counter. Ghislaine cursed under her breath and tried to ignore her mother-in-law's pale blue eyes and single gray whisker sprouting from her chin.

"Just lookin'," Blanche muttered. "Your eyes. They look funny. When's the last time you slept the whole night?"

"I'm sleeping fine," said Ghislaine.

"Uh-huh. You keep on sleeping *fine* and you'll be lookin' like me soon," Blanche said in a particularly thick drawl. "Where I come from the young ladies don't bounce back like you after a couple of kids. Wouldn't want you to waste it."

"I said I'm alright," Ghislaine snapped, wiping up the sugar with a sponge. Blanche had a tone that left her unsettled, almost as bad as the screaming that would inevitably come. She checked her watch. About an hour.

Ghislaine gulped her sugarless coffee. "I've got an errand. I'll be back after—...afterwards." She flicked the water on to rinse her cup and looked up suddenly. "Come with me today. We could go...to the mall, a coffee shop, wherever you want." The pleading in her own voice startled Ghislaine.

Blanche regarded her daughter-in-law. "Naw, you go ahead," she said finally. "I don't want to be a bother. You g'on and take care of what you need to take care of. I'll just listen to my music." She squinted across the kitchen counter, hurt that Ghislaine might only want her company as an excuse.

Ghislaine set the cup on a towel. "I'll have the girls when I get back. Maybe we can bring home some pizza?" she said scooping up her purse and keys.

"Fine," Blanche shrugged. She waited until Ghislaine got to the front door. "Tell Mr. Alex to save me some gin for the next poncy shindig."

Ohfuckohfuckohfuck she knows, Ghislaine's mind raced as she slammed the door and started the engine. ¡Pendeja! she cursed herself. How could she *not* have known? She might be old, but she's got eyes and ears and the *last* thing she is is stupid.

Ghislaine leaned forward to rest her head on the steering wheel.

The gentle vibration of the engine massaged her temple as Ghislaine remembered how her father would drag them to Doña Maritza. That's how she figured out the *curandera* had eyes for her father.

Doña Maritza had been doing readings for him, all of which predicted that—after a respectable period of mourning, of course—he would find another woman to love and provide for.

On the way home, he would brood.

"¿Qué tienes, Daddy?" Ghislaine asked after one particularly long visit.

"Nothing, m'ija."

"No, something's bothering you."

Her father shook his head and smiled out the window. "You know me, Ghilly. Sometimes I'm not sure who the real *curandera* is." He reached over and cupped her chin for a moment and then frowned again.

"Is it what that Doña Maritza keeps saying? About you finding another wife?"

He blew out a long breath. "Yup. It's getting a little hard to hear."

Ghislaine sensed an opening. "Then how come we keep going?"

Her father smiled tiredly at her and then stared at the freeway ahead. "Good question. *Eres bien lista, m'ija.* I don't know. She reminds me of...." He fell silent and frowned again.

"She's not Mami." Despite herself, Ghislaine heard the childishness in her voice and felt ashamed lecturing her father.

Ghislaine's father shot her a sharp look that couldn't completely conceal his embarrassment. "No! I know, *m'ija*. What I meant was, she's *certain*. There's a *confidence* in the things she says and," he shrugged feebly, "it helps."

Ghislaine looked up at her father, the man who had fought to be strong through her mother's illness, who had fought family to hold onto her when no one believed he could manage things without a woman. For the first time since her mother passed, Ghislaine watched his eyes spill over with tears.

"She can *see* things, *m'ija*," he said. "I need that right now. We need that."

"I can see things, too, Daddy, and I see that Doña Maritza shows lots of cleavage and wants you to keep coming back," Ghislaine said flatly.

"¡Ey!" her father grunted. Ghislaine stared at her shoes, cursing her own mouth. They drove in silence as her father wiped his eyes with the heel of his palm.

"Do we have to go back, Daddy?" Ghislaine asked. "Esa mujer no me cae bien."

"¿Cómo qué no te cae bien? Since when did you start sounding so grown up?"

Since the day Mami died Ghislaine wanted to say.

"Just one more time," he sighed. "Doña Maritza wants to do a cleansing on both of us. Just to make sure things are okay." Ghislaine's father watched her for a moment. "Have I told you how much your eyes look like your mom's? Amber, like a cat's."

"Lots of times, Daddy."

Ghislaine's father shook his head slowly. "What will those eyes see, *m'ija?*"

* * *

"If you hate me so much, why don'tcha go ahead and kill me?" he wheezed.

The wheezing was the worst. That and the oxygen tanks and tubes. The only upside was that the weaker Leonard got, the easier it was to handle his rages. Eventually they weren't even beatings, really—just furious pattings she could shrug off with barely a bruise. It was almost sad to watch. Almost.

He all but begged me to, Blanche reminded herself. Looked straight at me and said he wanted it. The pillow was right there, next to his head. He even closed his eyes when I put it over his face.

Blanche's fists grasped at dirt, the brittle pine needles stabbing her palms and poking through her thin nightgown. She'd ventured a short distance into the woods this time. Rather than fight the screaming head-on, she let it take her, *rode* it like she'd once ridden her uncle's horse, the one that never liked her and would chuff and swish its tail whenever she approached its stable. It knows about you, she thought. Let it kick and snort. Just don't fall off.

Isn't this what you wanted, traipsing into the woods like Red Riding Hood?

I had to see.

No, you could'a stayed at the house, curled up like a pillbug, listening to Patsy Cline or Doc Watson. You think this is somehow gonna make things right.

Nothing'll ever be totally right. That's just not how things work.

Then why'd you walk into the trees just before the reckoning? To punish yourself? Crying in the shower not enough for you?

Eventually the presence faded, as if it had tired of this game and moved on for now. Blanche rolled over in the pine needles, unsure how long she lay there after the screaming had subsided. Her head felt like an elephant had stomped it flat and her gut shook wetly. By some miracle she'd managed to keep from messing herself.

Gotta get back before Ghislaine and the girls, she thought. She stood shakily and looked upslope through the trees to where she was certain it came from. Shredded images of Leonard, his tongue lolling out of his slack mouth, spiraled away as she stumbled down the thickly wooded hillside, steadying herself on pine trunks.

We all got things, she thought.

At the edge of the woods, Blanche stopped and craned her neck to face the trees above her. Tomorrow, she promised herself, she would go all the way in.

* * *

Ghislaine welcomed the punishing sting of the mouthwash, the twenty-two percent alcohol kind. If I drank enough of this would I get drunk or throw up first? she wondered. Which would I deserve more?

She tried to convince herself that, from the neck down at least, she looked decent in the mirror. Her cinnamon-colored stomach was mostly flat with barely a hint of a pooch, and her small breasts had pretty much survived two ravenous children. Even so, she didn't bother wearing her lacy underwear. Nothing made her feel very desirable anymore. Her jog bra and cotton mom panties got him there just fine.

As long as she didn't look herself in the eyes—those amber eyes her father so admired and respected—she might convince herself that she still looked normal. The dark circles she could explain away. The kids' summer schedule, Carl never home, Blanche's wanderings and occasional public nudity, and the fucking fucking fucking screaming. A quarter of every day lost to it now, making her and most of Whitehill refugees until it was safe to come home. It's no wonder everything in the neighborhood is looking ragged, she thought. Including me.

But the purple bags were nothing compared to the eyes themselves. She'd always been proud of them, light mocha with flecks of gold near the center. But since the screaming started, it was as if some contagion had begun to spread outward from her pupils, a lifeless slick of blackness that had slowly wicked into her irises, stealing the light from them. Her Filipina roommate in graduate school had perfectly black eyes. On her they were beautiful. Here in Alex's mirror, they were utterly wrong.

Grad school. Back when I thought I was going to be something.

Ghislaine bent toward the mirror again and was shaken by a sudden memory of her father, next to her in their old Pinto and telling her she had her mother's eyes.

She spat the mouthwash into the sink.

"What have these eyes seen, Daddy?" she whispered. "Not enough? Too much?"

Ghislaine knew neither was true, that for too long she had seen mostly what she wanted to see. A fiction of a worthwhile life she'd convinced herself she wanted. "Not the children," she mouthed. But everything else—the money, the luxuries, Carl.

She steadied herself against the bathroom counter, closed her eyes, and remembered eggs.

＊ ＊ ＊

"C'mon, Ghilly. If you keep pouting like that, Doña Maritza will think you're giving her the *mal de ojo*."

"Maybe I am."

They listened to the *curandera* in the kitchen, preparing for the cleansing. Ghislaine fidgeted, her impatience growing by the second.

Doña Maritza entered the living room with a large tray holding two eggs and two glass bowls filled with clear water. Ghislaine couldn't help but notice the low cut of the *curandera's* blouse and how the woman's eyes repeatedly drifted to her father.

The *curandera* slowly moved the egg over her father who lay flat on the sheeted cot. Ghislaine tensed when she leaned forward to touch the egg to his forehead, imagined launching herself to claw at the woman's eyes should she try to steal a kiss or pull some similar stunt.

After several minutes, Doña Maritza withdrew the egg and cracked it three times against the lip of the bowl. Her heavily made-up eyes narrowed as she bent forward to inspect the yolky water. Ghislaine leaned in to better see for herself before the woman's withering glare forced her back into her seat.

Doña Maritza peered into the bowl, humming contentedly at what she observed. "I am pleased, Señor Trujillo, *very* pleased."

"What does it say?" Ghislaine asked, unable to contain herself.

The *curandera* frowned at Ghislaine before returning her attention to the bowl. "You're doing well, Robert."

Robert? Ghislaine bristled.

"Your spirit is mending quickly," Doña Maritza said in a silky voice. "Soon, very soon, you will be able to commit your heart once again to someone who deserves it."

Ghislaine gaped at her father who responded with a sly wink and eyeroll. *Tranquílate, m'ija,* she knew he was telling her. *Que tengas paciencia.*

When her time came, Ghislaine lay rigidly on the cot. The sheet smelled vaguely of the perfume, cologne, and body musk of previous customers. Doña Maritza swayed as she held the egg just above Ghislaine's skinny thirteen year-old body, the woman's voice crackling with urgency and her forehead suddenly beaded in sweat. Past the *curandera*, her father leaned forward, his posture rigid.

He doesn't like this, Ghislaine thought.

With a shudder, Doña Maritza turned uneasily to the second bowl of water. She pressed the egg to her lips, whispered some words, and struck it against the edge of the glass.

Into the bowl plopped a fetal chick, a red cloud of blood billowing through the water.

Ghislaine's father sprang from his chair. "¡Qué chingaos!" he spat, his face twisted in rage.

"Richard, I'm sorry. Your daughter...I'm so sorry."

* * *

"My, my, don't you look exotic," Alex said, leaning against the doorframe.

The burn of the mouthwash began to fade, but Ghislaine closed her eyes and kept working it through her teeth and around her tongue. She imagined the sweet slurry of chemicals, alcohol, and saliva washing away Alex, Carl, Whitehill. Everything. No, not everything. The twins deserve better from me, Ghislaine thought.

And Blanche. I hope she has her headphones ready.

Alex was still there when Ghislaine opened her eyes. She couldn't help letting them fall to his open robe. He was red, raw, and impossibly, ready again. She swallowed the last essence of mouthwash.

"You don't have to leave yet." he said.

She shot him an incredulous look. Since it started, Ghislaine had tried to convince herself that she fled the screaming for the girls' sake. She'd never hunkered down, hiding behind music or white noise, like her mother-in-law and some of her more masochistic neighbors. Standing in her underwear in Alex's bathroom, the screaming stalking closer every minute, she knew it was fear and shame that drove her to run like a thief from her own life.

"It's going to start soon," she said.

"Exactly," he smiled, fondling himself clumsily.

"Funny, Alex." Ghislaine saw what he was doing with his hand. "Wait, you're not joking. No. No way."

Alex grinned. "What are you afraid of? What people will think? Of hurting Carl? That he'll be *mad* at you? Scared of what you'll look like at your worst? News flash, sweetie: I've seen you at your worst and you're still pretty cute."

He held himself in his hand, almost fully there. "Come on, let's throw caution to the wind."

* * *

Ghislaine and her father sat side-by-side on the bench licking their cones.

The scene replayed in her head: her father pulling her from the cot and throwing money at Doña Maritza. Spanish words she'd never heard him use before bursting from his mouth as the *curandera* held her hands up and professed her innocence. Ghislaine's father didn't stop cursing until they'd pulled up to the ice cream parlor.

"Ghilly, *m'ija*, I'm so sorry I let her do that to you." His voice was calmer now, contrite. "I hope you'll forgive me."

Ghislaine looked up from her mint chip cone. "Daddy, the egg—"

"—was a trick, baby. It's easy to tell that there's a chick inside. She must've saved that one for you."

"Why me?"

"I think because she knew you didn't like her," he chuckled. "Because you saw through her."

"But—"

"Olvídatelo. Es una fraude, Ghilly."

"No, she said things would be hard for me, Daddy. She said I would struggle—that I would need help someday."

Her father squeezed her shoulder and sighed. "Ay, Ghilly,

toda la pinche vida is a struggle. All of it. If it weren't, there wouldn't be a reason for it."

* * *

"Ma'am, I need to ask you to please clear the street."

The police officer had pulled his cruiser to the curb and rolled down the window. Blanche appreciated that he didn't use the loudspeaker on her this time. "The disturbance will start up soon and we need everyone to either leave or get inside." Blanche continued her shuffle up the sidewalk, shadowed by the patrol car. "Ma'am," he said, his mirrored sunglasses glinting at her, "we can't have you collapsing in anyone's yard again." The cop checked his mirrors impatiently. "Ma'am, can I give you a ride? I need to clear out of here for the duration."

Blanche paused and approached the cruiser. "I remember you," she said as she lashed him with her wickedest grin. "You've seen me nekkid."

The cop's eyes widened behind his mirrored shades and he cleared his throat. "Well, I...."

"You run along," she laughed, leaning into the open window. "I'm just a block from home. Nobody gonna fuss with an old lady, and I'm too decrepit to do any harm."

The cop smiled back warily. "Alright, ma'am, but please get home a-s-a-f-p. Things have been getting worse around here. Seems like every week we have to do more clean up after the—" He peered up the hill through his windshield. "—after the disturbance."

Blanche followed the police officer's glance upslope. He was right, of course. After trying to maintain order the first few weeks, the authorities had largely abandoned the neighborhood for the six hours a day that it succumbed to the screaming. It did no one any good to have cops flailing in madness in their cruisers, their sidearms within too-easy reach during the onslaught. In the minutes after the screaming stopped, those who had stayed home would hold their heads, clean up after themselves, and wait for the sirens.

She had read the online debates over whether to post detailed descriptions of the deaths and accidents. What do I care if some stranger slits his own throat? someone wrote. But what if it wasn't suicide? another countered. What if there's a murderer taking advantage of the crisis? If there is, others said, then there's not just one.

Blanche wasn't afraid of murderers. She knew what murder looked and felt like. She'd seen enough to know that the reckoning was a torture custom-made for each and every person who experienced it.

She patted the hood of the cruiser. "Git. I'll see you tomorrow," she said and stepped back onto the curb. The cop shrugged and sped away with a wave of his fingers.

Blanche continued until she stood on the edge of the woods. She breathed in the murmur of the trees and began her uphill trek towards where she sensed it would be strongest. If you didn't live in this shit-for-soul neighborhood, she thought, you'd never know what's coming.

Wind hissed through the needles and slender trunks creaked all around her. She'd never been this far into the woods. Blanche marveled at the gloomy chill that filled the spaces between the pines on this otherwise warm, cloudless day. The darkness stretching between the trees seemed to her like a massive spider's nest capturing any light foolish enough to come too close.

With every step her resolve hardened. Somehow, she knew it was time to face what she had done to Leonard.

Soon, Blanche found herself in a small hollow. The area

was devoid of trees and the weak light seemed reluctant to penetrate the depression in the earth. At the first sign of that telltale mosquito-whine, Blanche lay flat on her back and closed her eyes.

* * *

The sight of Alex on his back, robe opened wide, made Ghislaine think of a flayed fish. Robotically, she crawled onto him and sat on his thighs. Above them a large ceiling fan blew thick air onto the bed. The breeze rustled Ghislaine's dark hair while her hands fumbled for him.

Afraid of what Carl would think? To *hell* with him! Ghislaine thought, the very idea causing her to pull harder. Never home. No idea what's happening with the twins. What they're feeling, how they miss him. All the late nights and travel. And not a care in the world for his own mother beyond providing room and board.

Straddling Alex, Ghislaine felt a pang of relief. Would I even care if Carl were screwing other women? Alex's hips bucked and she felt him throb between her fists. God, I actually hope he is, she thought.

She closed her eyes and tried to focus on anything but where she was.

In the farthest corners of her consciousness, it started—a high, ringing presence that gradually, painfully coalesced into shapes and flashes of images. Sharp leaves floating in a swimming pool, six blue jet planes pointing their fiery exhausts at her, tiny Blanche standing alone before a phalanx of brooding pine trees, her father's square-jawed face glowing with love as the force of the jet engines reached them behind the chain-link security fence.

"Daddy?" Ghislaine mouthed as she raised her face to the ceiling fan.

* * *

Memories swirled, trailed by whatever it was behind the screaming that Blanche knew was hurtling towards her.

Leonard's fingers tore at her arms, face, hair—anything within reach. Blanche could almost feel the pillow in her hands, arms and chest burning from exertion as her husband flailed with that desperate, near-end strength. The years of beatings, sorrow, anger. Suddenly, she was the stronger one.

"I'm sorry," she mouthed. "For you. For me."

Leonard's ashen, lifeless eyes hovered before her. Blanche could swear he smiled before his face, dead and gray against the white sheets, was torn away, the sheets curling ghost-like in the wind as he disappeared into the vortex.

Blanche's body jerked, rose into the air, and landed hard in the pine duff a few feet away. Stunned, she lay perfectly still, afraid that every bone in her body was shattered. Through the pain, Blanche wondered at the new silence that filled the hollow. She placed a shaking hand on her chest.

"It's gone," she gasped. "Gone!" In the time it took for the tears to line her cheeks, she felt release, a settling deep within that reminded her what it meant to be at peace. "Goodbye, Leonard," she said for the last time.

Blanche cautiously lifted her head and scanned the woods. I'm free, she knew. She wanted to laugh and give a middle finger to the gloom that now aimed its retribution at everyone but her. Her joy faltered. The rest—they're still in it, she realized. "Ghislaine," she said aloud as her own proud words betrayed her. *It don't seem right to run away.*

Blanche lay her head on the soft dirt and closed her eyes.

The muted screaming raged just outside her mind. Slowly, with trembling hands, Blanche reached out to open the door.

A poisonous breath of air moved over her. She sensed the onrush of lives, deaths, and regrets, tortures for sins and disappointments that were not hers. As the entirety of Whitchill's shortcomings and failures sped towards her, she forced herself open to accept them. "Ghislaine," she whispered just before her body rose again and the storm fell.

* * *

The darkened bedroom shook from the screaming. The headboard banged against the wall as the fan swayed on its rod above them, spinning blades threatening to tear into the ceiling.

A vein swelled across Alex's forehead. Ghislaine could hear his stomach lurch as she clamped down to keep from emptying herself. Alex's eyes rolled to white in a mash of agony and ecstasy.

Ghislaine tossed her head back again and tried to lose herself in the screaming. Her body vibrated so violently in response that she half-hoped she would come apart, piece by piece, scattered to the wind by the rush of anger and guilt.

Take me, asshole, she taunted. Turn me into nothing.

* * *

Blanche floated inches off the ground.

It all came too fast for her to hold back. She was the funnel through which Whitehill's tortures flowed. Every transgression, crime, slight, lie, omission, commission—anything that anyone had done to cause themselves or others anguish—flooded in: a withheld apology; a gambling addiction; an emptied trust fund; a father standing over his sleeping son, wrestling a demon his own father had thrust into him as a boy; a black eye blamed on a fall. And betrayals...too many to count.

Through the onrush a small blue dot expanded to the size of an ocean. In the water, a woman floated peacefully while a handsome, middle-aged man wiped away tears. Blanche fought the urge to judge, reminding herself of Leonard—until another image appeared.

A woman—small in stature, intense, anxious, like a tightly coiled spring.

This woman's regrets roared above the rest. Ashamed, Blanche tried to turn away, but could not. A young mother, born like her into a life very different from this. Ambition numbed by neglect, the sins of hopelessness, cynicism, and apathy dragging like chains from her soul.

* * *

Behind fluttering eyelids, understanding took shape in Ghislaine's mind.

A swimming pool. Blue-green water glittering beneath a punishing summer sun. Not this summer, she somehow knew. Last summer, when Carl had moved them to Whitehill. Honey locust leaves dotted the water. At first floating calmly, the pointed, canoe-shaped leaves began to bob and swirl. A panicked scream. Splashing. Another scream, "Alex! Stop! Please! Al—" A woman's voice. The leaves swirled in the agitated water until something new appeared on the edge of Ghislaine's vision: a woman's body, face-down, golden hair undulating in the sun-infused water. Beyond her, Alex stood waist-deep in the shallow end of the pool, his face flush from exertion and tears.

Ghislaine's muscles tensed. Without thinking, she clamped

onto Alex's throat with one hand, the other pulling harder between his legs. With every tug she felt him go more limp.

"You," Ghislaine said, her voice razor-edged and harmonizing with the screaming. "Kara. You, did it."

"What? Wait!" Alex choked. He writhed beneath Ghislaine, helpless against this slight woman's sudden strength. "I—had—to," he croaked. "For us."

Ghislaine's eyes widened as the realization took hold. "For us," she said through clenched teeth. "You killed her *for us?*"

Wet skin goosepimpled in the wash of the ceiling fan. Ghislaine's eyes darkened again and the room disappeared, replaced by a brilliant white sun shining into the car. Hot vinyl seats stuck to the back of her legs.

*   *   *

Her father was excited as they took the offramp to Moffett Field. She had never seen the Blue Angels.

They didn't have enough to pay admission, so he drove them down a service road and parked the car in the dry weeds at the south end of the runway. "Check it out, *m'ija,*" he pointed. "They'll taxi out here and then turn north, into the wind. Let all those losers waste twenty bucks to watch them from the stands. You'll never feel anything like this again, Ghilly."

Six blue and yellow fighter jets rolled towards them, turned about, and then crouched in arrowhead formation, their dual engine nozzles glowing molten orange. Her father pressed his hands over her ears and yelled something just before the twin maws of each aircraft exploded white-hot like dragon's nostrils. The noise and jet wash pummeled little Ghislaine. There was no hiding from the violence. She was turned inside out, all her secrets exposed to the punishing blast. Through her father's protecting hands the searing, strident note of the six jets combined to suck every ounce of dishonesty out of the atmosphere, leaving only naked truth: that she was her father's favorite person in the world, that she would do anything to maintain that status, and that the idea of disappointing him made her want to die.

Squinting into the heat-mangled space behind the jets, Ghislaine knew she would go on to make him proud.

The jets climbed out in tight formation and began to turn east, preparing for their first pass over the crowd a half-mile away. Breathless, Ghislaine looked up at her father.

"You see that, Ghilly?" he said in a trembling voice, tears lining his cheeks. "That'll be you. Strong and unpredictable. It'll be hard, but you'll find a way to do great things."

* * *

Ghislaine felt the muscles in her forearms bunch like steel cables beneath a layer of sweat. Alex twisted in pain from the screaming and Ghislaine's iron grip. Above them the ceiling fan swayed dangerously.

I put myself here, she admitted to herself. This man never forced me. I lowered myself to this. And Kara...

Ghislaine remembered the first time Alex and Kara had them over. The harmless flirtation, her hand on Alex's shoulder while she helped in the kitchen, smiles over her wine glass. It was fine. He's married and Kara's sweet, she'd told herself. It's just a little fun. Maybe Carl would even care enough to get jealous.

Oh my God, Kara. I'm so sorry.

* * *

Blanche accepted that she would die there, floating, filth running down her legs.

She forced herself to relax, to give in to it. Almost immediately the storm raging through her evened out, its howl becoming a single, high note. Riding that note, the sins of Whitehill residents familiar and unknown passed through and were ripped away, relegated to some nothingness that swallowed them whole, resolved for now.

A virtue slowly settled in Blanche's mind. Forgiveness. Through her, she thought, these sins might pass and enter some maw of resolution, a perfect blackness that ate their filth and rendered it irrelevant, a chance to start fresh.

As the screaming enveloped the neighborhood, louder than ever before, one woman's regrets and hatred fought the current and edged away from the event horizon of forgiveness.

Let it go! Blanche willed. Please, Ghislaine. Let me help.

* * *

The screaming roared through her now, as if a thousand Blue Angels carved formations through her brain. Ghislaine's body released. Shit, urine, and tears spilled onto Alex's thighs.

Fighting to remain conscious, Alex watched Ghislaine gaze upwards, slack-jawed at some private nightmare. Gasping through the vice on his neck, he forced his hands up Ghislaine's torso, inching them past her breasts to close around her slender throat.

Ghislaine stared upward through glittering black eyes. There was only one person who could understand any of this.

"Help me, Blanche," she mouthed.

Through the fan blades, Ghislaine caught jagged glimpses of Blanche floating in the dark woods. Her mother-in-law's face was contorted into a tortured rictus, thin body convulsing as blow after blow of some unseen force pummeled her. Blanche's face slowly rotated toward Ghislaine. The old woman's eyes opened and looked straight into Ghislaine's deepest parts, the way her father used to.

Alex's fingers tightened around Ghislaine's throat. Through the gap, Blanche looked into Ghislaine's heart, mouthing words her daughter-in-law could not hear, but knew nonetheless.

You'll find a way to do great things.

Ghislaine felt the words swell up from within, contending with her resentment of Carl, her fear of living on her own, her self-hatred for what she had allowed her life to become here in Whitehill. Here in Alex's bed. Over everything loomed the shame of what her father would have thought about it all.

Let me take it, dear, Ghislaine felt more than heard. *Let me do this one last thing for you.*

Swaying over Alex, Ghislaine's body quaked as her rage poured itself into Blanche, a simple peace steadily replacing the poison. With the clarity came an awareness of the tightening around her throat. Ghislaine flailed at Alex's neck with her free hand, but was unable to reach it again. She threw her head back and shrieked louder than the screaming itself. Through the fan blades Ghislaine saw Blanche's body spin faster, suspended mid-air in the dark woods. The bed shook and ceiling cracked as the fan wobbled dangerously above them.

Her arms pulled with every ounce of hatred and hope that remained.

* * *

The screaming had narrowed to a point so fine that it seemed impossible it wouldn't carve her into pieces, her mind and body diced into tiny cubes for the forest animals to scavenge. It felt good to serve a purpose at the end of things. Blanche's last thoughts before everything went dark were of her grandchildren and how things could be for them if Ghislaine could only forgive herself.

* * *

Ghislaine tumbled backward off the bed when Alex came free, a spray of flesh and blood splattering the fan blades. From where she landed on the floor, all she could see of Alex was his flailing legs and a repeating spout of blood erupting from his groin. Incredulous, Ghislaine's eyes focused past the bed to the far side of the room where the fan had batted a slick jumble of meat and hair.

She pushed herself away from the bed until she had backed up against a wall, the paint cool against her feverish skin. With a detached dread, Ghislaine watched Alex's manhood slowly slide down the window blinds. On the bed, one shaking hand searched the void where his groin used to be while the other reached out in vain for the window. A resigned mewl escaped Alex's lips when the blood-slick bundle pulled free from the blinds and fell in a lump to the carpet.

After several minutes, Alex lay motionless on the bed.

I should run, Ghislaine thought numbly. No, I should check on him. I need to check on him.

No sooner had she started to crawl toward the bed than a wisp of drywall dust appeared from above. With a crack, the spinning ceiling fan fell onto Alex's lifeless body sending more blood spraying across the room.

Ghislaine collapsed face down onto the carpet. Blanche, please take care of my daughters. Please, you crazy old woman, Ghislaine begged just before passing out.

* * *

She came to with her cheek pushed into the carpet. The screaming had stopped. Her throat ached and she could hear sirens in the distance. On the bed, Alex lay tangled in deformed fan blades, his bone-white skin splattered in various bodily fluids. Ghislaine gagged. Even an abattoir couldn't smell as foul as this.

She gathered her clothes and hurriedly dressed in Alex's bathroom, not bothering to wipe herself off. Something caught her attention in the mirror as she dressed. Ghislaine nearly fainted again. Wide amber eyes stared expectantly back at her.

She blinked at her reflection, wondering what it all meant. "I'm back, Daddy," was all she could think to say before running for the front door.

* * *

Ghislaine's pace slowed as she approached the house. A wiry figure, silhouetted by the late-afternoon sun, stumbled down the sidewalk toward her. The old woman collapsed into her arms. Together they lowered themselves onto the curb, hand-in-hand.

"You alright?" Ghislaine asked, reluctant to meet her mother-in-law's eyes.

"Mmm-hmm," Blanche nodded.

They sat quietly until Ghislaine sniffed. "No offense, but you smell like death."

"That's alright, sugar, 'cuz you smell about the same as always," Blanche said flatly. Ghislaine laughed and shook her head in admiration.

"Ah, there are those fierce eyes I remember!" Blanche grinned. "Been a while."

Ghislaine's smile broke. "Blanche, I... Alex—"

"Hush. I know how it feels, in my own way. I promise you, it'll be okay," Blanche said as Ghislaine wept softly into her neck.

A car skidded to a stop in front of them. Blanche recognized the officer from earlier. "You ladies alright?" he asked.

Blanche wrapped an arm around Ghislaine and pulled her close. "We're fine. You go and help the others. We got things covered here, young man." The cop gave Blanche a curt nod before pulling away.

The two of them watched as neighbors began to emerge from their houses, wide-eyed in the dusk. "I think this'll be the last day these folk have to deal with this mess for quite a while," Blanche muttered.

Ghislaine wiped the tears with her sleeve. "Everything's new," she said, looking around them. "Like we're starting over." Blanche nodded silently. They held one another for several minutes until Ghislaine sat up straight and frowned at the violet-orange sky. "I'm going to divorce Carl."

"Christ Almighty, 'bout time," Blanche said.

Ghislaine pulled away to regard her mother-in-law. "You're not mad?"

"*Mad?* Hell no! Been a long time comin' and you both been too blind to see it." Blanche sighed. "Look—I did my best by Carl. Threw that apple as far from the tree as I could. Even I couldn't know how far it would roll," she said, waving her hand at the neighborhood around them. "I love my son," she went on, a hint of sadness coloring her voice. "I kinda have to. But that don't mean I have to like him or that I think he deserves my granddaughters—or you."

Ghislaine looked over the woman she'd come to accept as her mother-in-law and now understood to be so much more.

"You're gonna need help with the kids," Blanche said.

TOMAS BAIZA

"And you're going to need a place to live," Ghislaine answered and kissed Blanche on her sun-spotted cheek.

The old woman closed her eyes and blushed. They sat until the sun began to hang and the shadows of the trees stretched across the yard. "C'mon," Blanche said. "Let's get washed up and collect my grandchildren from that fancy camp of theirs."

At the top of the driveway, Blanche motioned Ghislaine inside and lingered in the yard. She could smell herself plainly now. Fighting the temptation to rush for the shower, she paused to look up the hill at the woods. The green wall of pines stood tall as always, but the trees seemed sharper now, more in focus. Blanche lifted her face to the waning sun, her outstretched hands sifting a breeze that somehow signalled that the reckoning would, for now at least, allow Whitehill a measure of peace.

Blanche nodded at the woods and fairly bounded up the steps, eager to start something new.

13
HUNGERS

A plate of rice, beans, and my mother's turkey in steaming *mole poblano*. The tortilla comes whisper-close to the spicy chocolate sauce that's only slightly darker than Brenda Moreno's cinnamon skin.

"*Ey, 'pérate.* We need to talk."

I roll my eyes and stare at the plate, waiting.

"*M'ijo*, that's a good dinner, *¿qué no?*"

"Yes, Mom." I drop the fork. The flour tortilla is warm in my palm.

"Can you remember a time when you were ever hungry?"

I fold the tortilla between my fingers and close my eyes. Soft and velvety. I shift on my chair. Oh fuck, am I really fondling a tortilla in front of my mother?

"Yeah," I say. "'*Orita.*" *Right now.*

"No. I mean, *cuando tenías hambre* for real and you couldn't remember the last time you ate and weren't sure the next time you would?"

"Yes, I can!" I hate how my voice sounds. I hate being fourteen. I hate that my palm is getting all sweaty and if I keep squirming on my chair my mother will *know*.

Hell is a place where a wilting tortilla gives you a hard-on at the dinner table.

"No, you can't," she says. "Because you've never felt hunger, have you?"

"No—I mean yes. I'm hungry *right now*, Mom."

"How could you possibly know what hunger is?"

My fingers cling to the tortilla's fading heat. I can't stop thinking about it. Her. "I know, Mom."

I know because Brenda told Nicolás to fuck off and started eating lunch with me, not him, and then Nicolás, Alex, and Martin started calling me marica and bitch and joto, and all of Brenda's girlfriends just giggle at me when I walk by and one of them asked me why I haven't given it to her yet, and Brenda says tomorrow's perfect because her parents are working late late.

I want to shout everything, so that she'll know the truth. About me. About what's going to happen.

My mother's almond eyes narrow to slits. "How many times do I have to tell you, *m'ijo?* You have never known hunger." She runs a hand through thick, blue-black hair. For the first time I notice a faint stripe of gray just above her ear. She sighs and cups my cheek. Her palm is cool against my skin. "Daniel, when I was your age, I ate once a day if I was lucky. Your *abuelita* would come home from the cannery and maybe your *tías* and I would get a tin of tomatoes. Maybe even some eggs if the chickens were having a good week."

I think about my grandfather's chickens and how I only see them on Thanksgiving or some cousin's *quinceañera*. It never occurred to me that actual eggs could come from those scrawny things. Brenda's parents don't have chickens. They have a shar pei.

"Daniel," my mother says, her voice softer now. "Sometimes I think that I failed because you don't understand what it means to truly need."

I plunge the tortilla into the *mole*. A thin layer has congealed over the cooling sauce and it doesn't look so good anymore. *Need? How do you not understand how bad I need this?* I push the tortilla around the plate, swirling together the rice and beans and *guajolote*—and then I wonder if they use the weird-ass word *guajolote* at Brenda's house or if they just say *turkey* and then I wonder what the regular Spanish and not-Mexican word for *turkey* is and why do I know how to say *cock* and the *c-word* in Mexican but not the school-Spanish word for fucking *turkey?*

My mother tears off a piece of tortilla and flicks it in her mouth, her strong, Indian teeth quickly turning it to mush. "*Dale*," she says. Her eyes are moist and hint at a disappointment I think she was born with. "Go on. Before it goes cold."

14
ADELANTE

A spasm of guilt ripped through Daniel sixty miles east of
Ely, Nevada. He barely registered the whine of tires
over the rumblestrip just before his truck left the road at
seventy miles per hour. Even blinded by tears, Daniel knew the
wave that smashed into him had everything to do with the
Spam burrito his mother had made for him that morning.

$$* * *$$

"*No te olvides ésto, m'ijo.* For when you get hungry," his mother
said, handing him the foil-wrapped bundle. She wiped her eyes
in the predawn chill, next to the little pickup. Behind her,
Daniel's half-sister stood frowning.

Cami frowns when she's sad, Daniel told himself. She
cares. I know she does.

"And make sure to put gas in the tank," his mother gulped.
She lunged in to press her cheek hard against his. "You can be
so forgetful when your head's in the clouds."

"Knowing him he'll end up on Jupiter," Cami added.

"¿*En serio, Camila?* Now?" his mother hissed. She led Daniel to the sidewalk and pulled his head down to hers. Daniel began to cry when she began to whisper into his ear.

* * *

He crossed the San Joaquin Valley beneath a crushing homesickness.

Wasn't this supposed to feel better? Didn't doing this show character? Maybe a little bit of guts?

Daniel didn't think that trips to San Francisco, Modesto, or Tijuana officially counted as 'travel.' And he'd never been away from family before. It wasn't until this summer that he realized he'd been raised with the South Bay conceit that the world came to you and so there was little need to go into the world.

You could hear all the accents you wanted from the kitchen window.

The highway bent upward as the familiar black oak and eucalyptus foothills gave way to dark, pine-covered mountains. Daniel remembered his mother's warning and stopped for gas at the resort in Kirkwood, staring open-mouthed at the granite mountains above him while the tank filled. He knew from his junior-year Earth Sciences class that these mountains owed their existence to the Farallon Plate's 200-million year nose dive beneath the continent. The rich kids at school—the ones who spent weekends skiing and came back smiling on crutches—never seemed to give two shits about plate tectonics. Standing there in the cold elevation, the beauty of these mountains, the idea of massive, unseen forces hundreds of miles beneath his Chuck Taylors pushing these mountains higher, shocked and humbled him.

"If I've never actually *seen* anything past the Sierras, does it really exist?" Daniel said out loud as he slammed the door of the truck. He half-expected a response from the passenger side of the bench seat. Nothing. Just an atlas, plastic water bottle, and a foil-wrapped burrito.

* * *

Who is it that can tell me who I am?

Daniel's eyes passed over the line again and again until King Lear's words were torn from his hands. He knew it was foolish to let himself get distracted on the way home from the bus stop. The Shakespeare anthology was too big and heavy for his backpack.

"Think you're special, fucking schoolboy?" Manuel pushed his forehead into Daniel's. His breath stank of Skoal and MD 20/20. Over his shoulder, Eddie and David elbowed one another, excited for the coming beatdown. "Bitch ass uniform," Manuel sneered, flicking Daniel's starched collar. "The priests make you suck their *pitos*, too?"

The blow landed so cleanly, Daniel's knuckles didn't even hurt when they crushed Manuel's nose.

The tall boy fell to the pavement, a thick slurry of snot and blood gushing through his fingers. Eddie and David stepped back when Daniel moved to pick up the book. Heart galloping, he repeated his mother's word for when things looked bad. *Adelante, adelante, adelante...*

"*¡Jódete, culero! ¡Pinche bolillo!*" Manuel gagged through the blood.

"*Ya estuvo,* Manny," Eddie said.

"Yeah, bro. Let it go," David piped in. "You can't fight crazy."

Adelante, adelante, adelante, Daniel repeated as he walked away.

* * *

Just as the trucker's atlas suggested, there was indeed a world beyond California. At Carson City, Daniel turned east onto Highway 50. Peering through the bug-smeared windshield, he was certain that the barren plain of central Nevada must be where Mars rovers were field tested and decrepit mariachis sent into oblivion when their arthritic fingers could no longer manage "El Niño Perdido" on trumpet.

An occasional sign mangled by shotgun pellets would remind him that he traveled *The Loneliest Road in America*. Rusted barbed wire. Splintered fence posts. Sun-battered sage. Twisted bitterbrush. Dirt roads that intersected the highway at ninety-degree angles and disappeared over the horizon. The only things missing were sahuaros and Roadrunner and Coyote.

Daniel wondered where those eerily straight roads could possibly go. To nothing, he thought—and then doubted that Father Benítez would have accepted the idea that any road or path could ever lead to nothing. He imagined the Jesuit wagging his finger at him during one of their talks. "If your road takes you nowhere," Father B might say, "then it's probably because you didn't actually want to go anywhere." Daniel rubbed his eyes and twisted the radio dial for anything other than preachers or pedal steel guitars. He was pretty sure he would give his left testicle for just one Metallica song out here in the middle of nowhere.

* * *

"This is it, gentlemen," Father B said in their last Philosophy class before graduation. "The end that is a new beginning."

In the fall, almost all of them would start college somewhere.

Daniel liked his Philosophy class. It was where he got to think big thoughts without feeling self-conscious. He also liked that Father B rocked a leather jacket around campus and listened to the Rolling Stones in his office. He'd begun meeting with the old priest freshman year, after his first fight in the cafeteria.

Father B walked slowly through the classroom. "Some of you will take paths that have been laid out for you. Others?" he said, resting the tips of his fingers on Daniel's desk without looking at him. "Others, will explore places for which you have no frame of reference." He tapped lightly on the desk before moving on. "What will that journey draw out of you? How will you use it to become you?"

* * *

Cami was beside herself when she found out.

"*Michigan?* May as well call it *Me-chingan!* Why there, Dani?" Cami asked, hands in the air. "You also got scholarships to Berkeley and Stanford. God, even *UCLA* would have been better!"

It seemed the only things he and Cami had in common were their mother and a principled contempt for SoCal.

"I heard it's so humid there it's like living in someone's mouth. And leaving me alone with Mom..." Cami trailed off, a deep worry line cutting into her brow. Daniel wondered how long after he left before that frown became permanent. "Just like Bill."

Daniel rounded on Cami and just as quickly clapped his hands over his face to hide the shame. To invoke Bill's name at a time like this... Only then did Daniel understand the full extent of Cami's anger. Her hatred for his White father was almost supernatural in its intensity.

Could I possibly be like Bill? he wondered. How do you tell the only family you've ever known that you need to experience something different? Is leaving home betrayal?

"You must really want to get away from here. Only *gabacho* kids move away from home just like *that*," Cami said, snapping her fingers in his face. "Guess that settles it, huh?"

* * *

"I had a good time, Daniel. For such a big guy, you're actually a pretty good dancer—once I could pry you off the bleachers." Wendy laughed, her eyes sparkling in the dark car. "I'm glad that we got paired up."

"Me, too," Daniel said as they took the off-ramp to Los Gatos.

The car rumbled confidently and he silently thanked Cami, as much as it galled him. "There's no freaking way I'm letting you take one of those fancy prep-school girls to prom in Mom's hooptie pickup," Cami had moaned, her eye roll approaching lethal intensity. Daniel had no idea how she convinced her latest boyfriend to give up his car for the night. But, just then, it didn't matter as the restored Barracuda's dual exhaust bumped like double-bass drums and the shift knob vibrated menacingly in his palm at the stoplight.

For maybe the first time in his life, Daniel was within spitting distance of cool.

He didn't know this side of the Valley well, but Wendy lived close to the private girls academy that often planned events with his all-boys school, so he was just familiar enough with that neighborhood to have picked her up and get her home. His most popular classmates had dates to senior prom all lined up in advance—some of them probably from birth, he figured. But people like him, the un-cool, had to enter a lottery where they were randomly paired with some similarly under-whelming specimen from the girls' academy.

Daniel had resigned himself to entering the lottery for as shy as he was. Wendy, though, he couldn't figure it out. With that smile and personality, there was no way someone like her should have struggled to find a prom date.

"Can I tell you a secret?" she said in a stage whisper. "Several guys from your school asked me to prom."

A shot of irrational jealousy ricocheted through Daniel.

"But, how do I say this...they all seemed like handsy, mouth-breathing douches who'd end up sucking on my pepper spray, so I decided I'd try the luck of the draw instead. And it worked!" She laughed with no hint of sarcasm or irony. "Ugh, this princess shit is uncomfortable," she said, torquing her neck and tugging at the high neckline of her gown.

Daniel's heart swelled. Beyond his wildest expectations, they were actually having a good time. He swallowed hard and when the light changed dropped the clutch a little too quickly. The Barracuda's rear tires howled. The shining car shot through the intersection with Wendy screaming out the open window and Daniel sawing at the steering wheel to keep them from fishtailing into the light pole.

"Whoa, Daniel! You're quiet, but you drive even better than you dance!"

* * *

The suede hardpan slid past. Mind-numbing desert endlessness. Daniel thought of Cami and then looked at himself in the rearview mirror for the hundredth time that day.

Only gabacho kids move away from home just like that, Cami had said.

* * *

"Do your parents know we're here?"

Daniel glanced nervously around the foyer of Wendy's massive Los Gatos house. He hadn't really noticed it when he picked her up because her parents were gushing, all the frenzied pictures, and she looked so beautiful in her dress. Gaping at the high ceiling and mission-style chandelier, it slowly dawned on him that Wendy might actually live in a mansion.

"Their room is all the way on the other side." Wendy smiled as she put Daniel's hand on her waist. She placed her hand on his shoulder and began to turn slowly, dancing to imaginary music. "A bomb could go off out here and they'd sleep right through it."

"A pin drops in our kitchen in the middle of the night and my mom's running around with her gun yelling about robbers," Daniel said quietly, his voice slightly hoarse. He could feel his heartbeat in his ears. The blue crêpe silk of Wendy's dress slid beneath his fingers. Her hip was round and firm.

"Ha! Your mom sounds awesome. My parents would just hide in the safe room and sip wine until the police showed up." She looked up at Daniel through half-closed eyes, her lips parted slightly. "So," she whispered, "I'm not really down for anything super heavy, you know, but...maybe something?"

Daniel's scalp began to tingle, a cold dread rising in the pit of his stomach. He'd figured this would happen someday. Wendy slipped her fingers under his cummerbund and gently pulled him up against her. "We could still have some fun before you go."

* * *

Noises from the kitchen told him he was not the first one awake. His mother stood at the stove in her floral print nightgown, her short, compact shape moving efficiently to manage a frying pan and two steaming pots.

Daniel took in the aroma of his mother's chile colorado. He had never learned how to make it like her. Albóndigas, mole poblano, huevos con chorizo, chile verde—he learned his mother's recipes so well even Cami couldn't compete. But the chile colorado had always eluded him. There was a magic that he couldn't conjure from the deep red sauce like his mother.

It has to be the cumin, Daniel thought.

He gently nudged her aside and took over at the stovetop. In the black iron skillet was a can's worth of cubed Spam bubbling in chile. She had taught him to turn the Spam at just the right rhythm—too quickly and you'd end up with mush, too slowly and it would burn. He turned his head to keep from inhaling the pepper fumes rising from the pan.

His mother grinned. *"Ya sabías que nuestra gente—"*

"Yeah, I know, Mom," Daniel coughed, blinking through watery eyes. "Our ancestors held their kids over burning chiles as punishment." She snickered and Daniel wondered whether he deserved to be punished for leaving.

At exactly the right moment he scooped the fried Spam onto the large flour tortilla his mother had laid out and prepared with spiced black beans and potatoes. Daniel had seen his mother fold a thousand tortillas and it always left him in frustrated admiration. When he did it, a stray kernel of rice or errant frijol would escape and require herding. His mother's tortillas, on the other hand, were perfect. Always.

They lingered in the kitchen until Daniel acted like it was sleep he wiped from his eyes. "I'm gonna start loading the truck," he said, leaning in to kiss the thick salt-and-pepper hair spread across her forehead. She smelled like warmth and home.

His mother nodded and turned quickly back to the stove.

* * *

Daniel had driven almost the length of Fallon when he remembered about the gas. He didn't technically need to fill up yet, but his mother echoed in his head along with Cami's jab that he'd end up on another planet if he wasn't careful. With a jerk of the steering wheel he pitched the little pickup truck into the last gas station in town.

Do they think I'm *gabacho* now? Under a white sun, he watched the digits slowly tally the gallons and dollars on the pump. Do we not get to go places, too? Why should I have to stay home to be me? What does 'being me' even mean?

Daniel hesitated before getting back into the truck. The tin foil bundle glinted in the sun blazing through the windshield. He couldn't shake the feeling that something waited for him in the cab. *Get in*, it purred. *Just another 2,100 miles to Ann Arbor—or 300 miles back home. You decide.*

He slipped behind the wheel, sweat beginning to bead on his forehead. A gaudy procession of fast food joints slid past on his way out of town. His mother would have sneered. *"M'ijo, when you're there, make sure to eat well. And stay away from junk like chicharrones!"*

"I don't think they have chicharrones in the dining hall, Mom."

"¿¡Te imaginas!? A place without chicharrones!"

* * *

On the way back from the kitchen, Daniel stopped in the dim hallway to inspect the family photos he'd ignored for years. He looked closely at the one of himself at age two, smiling proudly in his giraffe-patterned footie pajamas. Oh, man. And the one at eleven. An acne-ridden, pubescent, Picassoesque monstrosity with Carlos Santana curls and broad Mexican teeth pushing the limits of his braces. "Jesus Lord," he mumbled.

The other frames displayed his and Cami's annual school photos, with pictures of their mother mixed in. Over the years his mother's thick, black hair had become shorter and grayer, while Cami's had grown longer and more glamorous as she transformed from a sullen dork into a curvy bombshell with blue-black Farrah Fawcett hair and a tattooed beauty mark on her cheek.

The only thing consistent across the years of photos was that Daniel was by far the tallest and lightest of all them.

* * *

The road rippled in the stupefying heat. He checked the temperature gauge and felt some relief. It wasn't exactly a looker, but the truck ran well.

The previous winter his mother had insisted that they browse the used car lot.

"Why we need a truck, Mom?" he asked, walking between two dented Chevys still wet from rain.

His mother shrugged with that tilt of the head that Daniel knew from junior-year Rhetoric class was a lie of omission. She pointed at a Mazda mini-pickup that had seen better days. "What do you think, *m'ijo?*"

He smirked. "I think this one," he said, pointing at a slightly less-old Ford. "It's only $200 more. We've never had a car with air conditioning, Mom."

"*Uy, no*," she said, wagging her finger. "Too expensive."

* * *

For the next two hours, Daniel fought sleep while the heat shimmers danced across the two-lane highway. Between head bobs, he would peek at the foil bundle and the plastic water bottle next to it. Outside, the mirages quivered and swirled into the shapes of arrows or hands. Some beckoned him forward, others back. The phantoms crowded his windshield until he couldn't see past the end of the hood.

"*Fuuuck!*" he shouted at the heat itself, sweat dripping into his eyes. Daniel opened the bottle, splashed warm water onto his face, and stuck his head out the open window. The hot wind flung the water from his face, like slobber off a dog. It helped. The asphalt still folded and swayed in the afternoon heat, but the spirits had fled. The sharp perfume of heated sage and rabbitbrush filled his head.

* * *

"Shitshitshitshit. What's wrong? What can I do?"

Daniel felt Wendy next to him on the bed. His eyes were closed tightly, the tears salty on his lips. He shook his head and waved his hand to indicate that everything was fine, there was no problem, nothing to see here. He knew it was hopeless, that Wendy would see him plainly now.

"Here, sit up." Wendy's voice projected a calm authority that both embarrassed and centered him. Daniel swung his feet onto the floor and slouched over to hide his face.

"Hey," she said, placing a hand on his shoulder, "I really

need to get out of this thing—like, right now. It suddenly feels pretty stupid. You're upset and I'm all in this fucking princess gown."

Daniel bent over to bury his face in his hands. Sounds of Wendy moving behind him to the dresser. "I won't look. I promise. I'm sorry. I am so, so sorry." He rocked back and forth, as if the motion would somehow absorb the shame.

"Don't apologize!" she said between grunts as she wriggled out of her gown. "I'm worried I did something wrong, that I hurt you."

Daniel could only shake his head as he worked to steady his breathing, the way Father B had taught him. "No. It's not you." *In, one-two-three. Hold. Out, three-two-one.* "I—I didn't mean to scare you. I just...panicked. I guess."

The bed settled again and Daniel felt a hand under his chin gently turning his face. He opened his eyes. Wendy's formal makeup contrasted heavily with her 49ers t-shirt and sweatpants. "No, I'm the one who's sorry. I just assumed...." She searched his face, her lips tight.

"Assumed what?"

Wendy reached down to squeeze his hand and gifted him with a look. Daniel knew that, even though they had met through a lottery, had only spoken on the phone twice, and had met in-person only a few hours ago, this girl's concern was real. Daniel felt something that he had never felt with anyone his age. Trust.

"What did you assume?" he asked again.

Wendy cocked her head slightly and leaned in close to him. "Daniel, can I ask you something—I mean, no judgement?"

He smiled and squeezed her hand back to let her know that it was okay, that it might as well be now. That maybe he was ready.

"Go ahead. What do you want to know?"

* * *

Father B flicked the glass drinking bird he kept on the corner of his desk. It bobbed forward to sip from a matching shot glass and then rocked back, the green-tinted water flowing down its fluted body.

"Some booster sent me this as a gift," the priest said, shaking his head. "Apparently he figured a life of celibacy and service to God and his children merited this *chingadera*."

Daniel smiled. He liked it when Father B cursed. It made him more approachable. "You did take a vow of poverty," Daniel said under his breath.

The priest leaned back and laughed, his ample belly shaking beneath his black button-up shirt. "Smart ass," he said, catching his breath.

They both welcomed this break. Their talk had become serious and lasted far longer than usual, especially after Daniel had shared what happened with Wendy.

Father B straightened his shirt and sat upright again. He looked thoughtfully at the bobbing bird. "Daniel, I've dedicated my life to the Church and to those who seek peace through its teachings. At the same time, my order has established itself as a theological pain in the ass for its tendency to go off script."

Daniel sat stone-still, hanging on every word.

Father B smiled vaguely, inspecting the bird. "I want you to know that when it comes down to it, I'm here for you, regardless what the Church might say about any of it. Doctrine should serve people, Daniel, not the other way around." He paused for Daniel to say something, anything.

The boy sat, impassive as ever.

The priest sighed. "I know you better than maybe anyone else in this school. Once I established that you weren't a menace, I came to appreciate you as a horrible technical practitioner of Catholicism and an outstanding spirit. Behind that inscrutability is a loving person dedicated to giving more than he takes—with some minor hiccups along the way," he added.

Daniel's scalp prickled in embarrassment. He'd come for guidance, not compliments.

"You have the soul of an explorer,," Father B said. "This is just one more thing to make the expedition more interesting."

* * *

The little truck climbed into pinyon-juniper highlands. Father B had made them read Edward Abbey sophomore year. Daniel wondered whether the hiker who died of dehydration in *Desert Solitaire* sat beneath one of those kinds of trees in his last moments. Looking out over the mountainside of short, handsome conifers, he figured he agreed with Abbey that there would be worse ways to go. He glanced at the trucker's atlas spread across the steering wheel and traced the red line of Highway 50 eastward.

He was starving—and still so far from Eureka.

* * *

"When are you leaving, Daniel?" Father B asked. They had arranged to meet one last time after graduation.

"Two weeks," Daniel said. "I'll show up just in time to find my dorm and get my classes." He wondered if he would have time to write Wendy before classes started. How long would it take a letter to get to Princeton?

They sat for a while in silence. This time it was the priest who waited.

"I don't know why I'm doing this," Daniel blurted out. "I don't have any of this figured out yet. Maybe I should wait."

Father B leaned back and grinned. "Daniel, if we waited until we knew it all, we'd never go anywhere. We'd be like the band that never leaves the garage to play a real gig. Like the self-loathing writer who keeps revising and never actually submits anything."

Daniel let that sink in. He wondered whether anyone ever went out there feeling finished—or if they ever should. Maybe feeling like you've got it all figured out meant you were delusional. Or dead.

* * *

Daniel steered the truck through a narrow river gorge. Stray thoughts of his mother, Father B, Cami, and Wendy flashed so vividly in his head that he hardly noticed when the rock walls opened onto Ely. He almost ran the red at 5th Street and spared only a glance at the six-storey brick structure with the sign announcing HOTEL NEVADA–A NEVADA LAND-MARK SINCE 1929.

Highway 50 spit the truck out the east end of town. In the distance, a mountain his atlas called Wheeler Peak rose out of the plain. He tried to smile. The temperature was falling and the wide sky had taken on a surreal, purplish wash. His mood teetered on a precipice in the high-desert gloaming.

Daniel's stomach growled loudly enough to startle him. He had resisted his hunger not to save money, but to hold onto the last thing his mother had given him. Another grinding moan from his empty stomach. It's time, he thought.

* * *

The little pickup backed out of the driveway onto the street. Daniel hesitated, the engine idling quietly. His mother waved first. Cami put her arm around her, wiped her face, and shook her hand in the air, like shooing away a fly. Daniel watched them in his side view mirror until they disappeared in the twilight.

* * *

It all happened at once
the dash cluster, gas gauge, the needle pegged on E

sixteen-gallon tank, 258 miles between Fallon and Ely, sixty miles past Ely, averaging 21 mpg—

as his teeth cut through the tortilla.

The emotions pummeled him harder than Manuel ever did, an instantaneous overflow of guilt, grief, memory.

Somehow the little truck stayed upright as it spun through the gravel turnout and came to rest in a cloud of dust. Daniel stumbled from the cab and sprinted into the desert. Gnarled sage and bitterbrush snagged his t-shirt and jeans. Images flashed before him.

Mom
Cami
Wendy
Father B

On his right the looming silhouette of Wheeler Peak jabbing upward to tear a hole in the painted sunset. Jet engines roared through his head. Still clutching the burrito, he instinctively took another bite.

Pain ripped through him again. Tortilla, beans, potatoes, and cubed Spam spilled as he fell.

Face-down in the dirt, Daniel cursed through clenched teeth. He grabbed fistfuls of sand and pushed his forehead into the ground. At some point, the tears dripping off his nose, he passed out.

* * *

Cool desert sand rasped Daniel's cheek. He couldn't tell how long he'd been there. Long enough to have started shivering.

His mother's words in the driveway echoed and looped back over themselves. "Dani, *escúchame bien*" she whispered in his ear, "we've known for a long time that this would happen. *Nos resultó útil la troca ¿qué no?* I know you feel bad about leaving. It's okay! I'll have my hands full with your sister, believe me. And please don't worry about Cami. She will never totally forgive me for Bill. I'm sorry that sometimes she blames you, too. If you want, blame me. I made a bad choice that she and I live with, but what hurt me and Cami also gave me you. *Así pasan las cosas ¿eh?* The good with the bad. It's time," she said, patting his cheek. "*M'ijo*, whoever and whatever you become out there, we love you. No matter what. And when things get hard, *que sigas adelante.* You hear me? Not backwards. *Adelante.*"

He rolled onto his back and gazed into the darkening sky. The faint births of stars above, like the slow opening of eyes looking down on him. "Thank you, Mom," Daniel said to one particular point of light. It glowed more than sparkled. He thought of Cami and wondered whether it was Jupiter.

The dust had settled by the time Daniel got back to the truck. Sliding into the cab he sensed both opportunity and an overwhelming sense of responsibility.

"Sixty miles west to Ely," he said, patting the dashboard. "Definitely won't make it that way."

TOMAS BAIZA

The engine turned over on the first try. Daniel eased the truck back onto Highway 50, eastbound and short-shifting to preserve the last drops of gas.

Daniel grasped the wheel with clammy hands, not certain who he was about to become. With the needle tapping E, a single word repeated in his head like a mantra.

Adelante.

ABOUT THE AUTHOR

Tomas Baiza was born and raised in San José, California, and now lives in Boise, Idaho, where he is currently studying creative writing at Boise State University. Tomas is a Pushcart-nominated writer whose work has appeared or is forthcoming in *Parhelion, Writers In The Attic, Obelus, In Parentheses, Meniscus,* [PANK], *101 Proof Horror, The Meadow, Peatsmoke, The Good Life Review, Ordinary Madness,* Black Lawrence Press, *Storyfort* 2020/21, and elsewhere.

Earlier versions of these stories first appeared in:

• **"And Then A Wind"** *Parhelion Literary Magazine,* Issue #5 (July, 2019)
https://parhelionliterary.com/tomas-baiza/
REPRINTED: *fresh.ink* (June 29, 2020)
https://fresh.ink/magazine/8157

• **"Hole"** *Writers In The Attic: FUEL* (August, 2019).
Competition sponsored by The Cabin (Boise, Idaho).
Judge: J. Reuben Appelman (*The Kill Jar*). PRINT ONLY.

• **"A Purpose To Our Savagery"** (originally "Wolves")
Obelus Journal, Issue #1 (December, 2019). Featured story of first issue.
https://obelusjournal.com/content/wolves/

- **"Come Stai, David?"** *In Parentheses Literary Magazine,* Issue 4, Volume 5 (April, 2020) https://inparenthesesmag.wordpress.com/2020/04/15/first-look-in-parentheses-magazine-spring-2020-crowds-edition/?fbclid=IwAR3hBmPtk4Ht7CQZstNmpC6NZKmmkXKoXzTvRny_bSUJ-SQyP7fj68XoO2o

- **"Love Ritual"** (poem) *Meniscus Literary Journal,* Volume 8, Issue 1 (May, 2020) https://www.meniscus.org.au/Vol8Iss1.pdf

- **"A Reckoning"** *100 Proof Horror Anthology* 2020 (July, 2020) http://hauntedmtl.com https://amzn.to/3hIXdHS

- **"Stud"** [PANK] *Magazine,* #LatinxLit Celebration Issue w/audio narration (July, 2020) https://pankmagazine.com/2020/07/28/latinxlit-tbaiza/

- **"Nezahualcóyotl"** *The Meadow* (Fall, 2020). https://www.tmcc.edu/flipbook/meadow/2020/

- **"Extra-Large For The Lord"** *The Good Life Review* (Fall, 2020) https://thegoodlifereview.com

- **"Adelante"** *Peatsmoke Literary Journal* (Fall, 2020)—**2020 Pushcart nomination** https://www.peatsmokejournal.com/fall-2020-fiction/adelante

• **"A Seal's Song"** *Fire & Water: Stories from the Anthropocene* (Black Lawrence Press, August, 2021)
https://www.fireandwaterstories.com

RIZE publishes great stories and great writing across genres written by People of Color and other underrepresented groups. Our team consists of:

Lisa Diane Kastner, Founder and Executive Editor
Mona Bethke, Acquisitions Editor
Rebecca Dimyan, Editor
Abigail Efird, Editor
Laura Huie, Editor
Cody Sisco, Editor
Chih Wang, Editor
Pulp Art Studios, Cover Design
Standout Books, Interior Design
Polgarus Studios, Interior Design

Learn more about us and our stories at www.runningwildpress.com/rize

Loved this story and want more? Follow us at www.runningwildpress.com/rize, www.facebook.com/rize, on Twitter @rizerwp and Instagram @rizepress